BLIND MAN'S BLUFF

A MYSTERY

E. RICHARD JOHNSON

By the same author

BLIND MAN'S BLUFF

········ **A** ········
MYSTERY

E. RICHARD
JOHNSON

A Joan Kahn BOOK

St. Martin's Press
New York

Design by John Fontana

Library of Congress Cataloging-in-Publication Data

Johnson, E. Richard, 1937–
  Blind man's bluff.

  "A Joan Kahn book"
  I. Title.
PS3560.O376B5 1987   813'.54   87–15999
ISBN 0–312–00999–2

A Joan Kahn Book

First Edition

10 9 8 7 6 5 4 3 2 1

For Kathy and the pep talks.

BLIND MAN'S BLUFF

·······A·······
MYSTERY

E. RICHARD
JOHNSON

1

The morning rush was over when he left the small coffee shop.

The rush hour's frantic din had changed into the settled roar of a city at work. On the sidewalk, he lifted his face to the east, feeling the warmth of the sun and the promise of another hot day. Thoughtfully, he opened the collapsible white cane he carried and felt his way to the curb. He began walking toward the row of apartment buildings up the block.

In this part of the city there were not many pedestrians on the sidewalk during the morning hours, usually only a few women from the neighborhood on their way to some early shopping at the corner market. During the evening hours a casual walk was more difficult. Between eight and midnight the block was swarming with young hookers working the night traffic, and pushers selling a night's worth of dreams.

Even the smells were different during those evening hours, he mused. Now, there was the burning odor of car exhaust that was always present, mixed with breakfast aromas like fresh coffee and the stale odor of old booze and sour vomit creeping out of the alley he passed.

It was better at night, he supposed. No, not better, just *different*. Well, at least at night the sounds and smells were more alive—the click of high heels and the scent of cheap perfume. One girl always wore a fragrance that reminded him of newly cut cedar, a fresh, clean scent, like that found in the Big Sky country of Montana.

He could remember days that he had spent there, long, quiet days, when the mountains looked close and the land seemed to lie flat, right up to the blue foothills. Days when he could spend hours riding and not see more than one or two ranch houses. The country had never changed. Each time he had returned to it, it had been the same—big, quiet, and restful.

At the corner, he waited until the squeak of brakes told him the cross traffic had stopped before he proceeded.

Once this was over, he decided, he would buy the best dog available, one that could take him anyplace in the city. But he'd have to be a dog that would like ranch life, too— not some dumb pup that would get his head kicked off by the first horse he met. A dog would afford some protection on the city's streets; people gave you some room on the sidewalk then. But once they had the money, he wouldn't need to worry about getting around the city, he would go back home and find a ranch to buy.

He'd always dreamed about that, and the dream had kept him going for eight years now, ever since he'd returned— first, during those bad years when they had put him back together. He'd had problems with the doctors then. They seemed to hold him responsible for getting caught in the shelling that had killed most of the platoon. It didn't matter

2

that he had been following orders like the rest of the guys, or that the rest of the company had been chopped up, too. The doctors sometimes acted as if they resented the fact that he had lived and that now they had the responsibility for returning him to a life as normal as one could expect, considering what he had left behind on the shelled land.

It had seemed to take his body forever to heal and his mind to adjust to the new reality of living in perpetual darkness. There had been some bad years, and the thing that had kept him going was the thought of the money, not the lousy little disability check they gave him, but real money, enough to buy the biggest ranch in Montana!

He reached the familiar phone booth in front of his apartment building and felt his way to its door, turning sharply to be lined up with the entrance. He felt a sense of relief when he was sure the entranceway and steps were free of loiterers. Around here, being blind was no guarantee against muggers and beatings.

Hell, in this neighborhood being old and crippled or defenseless was almost a guarantee of being attacked during some hours of the day. So even a blind man was fair game. But inside the building there was a measure of safety.

He closed the foyer door and relished the cool air, noticing as well the faint odor of age the building carried, as though it had lived beyond its time. He climbed quietly upstairs to his apartment and unlocked the door. Entering the apartment, he closed the door behind him, and as it clicked shut he realized suddenly that someone else was there.

He sensed a presence, then detected the faint odor of a cigarette. He took another step and was struck by the stench of stale sweat and was certain someone stood close by him. He experienced a surge of fear and began to open his mouth to shout for help. He drew breath to yell, and something hard smashed against the back of his head. As he fell, he

3

wondered how anybody could have discovered his secret. He crumpled to the worn rug and lay unmoving.

The man stood over him, listening carefully to the silence of the building for long minutes before he dragged the body to a wooden chair and sat the unconscious man down and began to tie him into it.

Patrolman Packer had used the potted plant in the hall to throw up in. All things considered, it had been one hell of a bad day. Two muggings, a purse snatching, three simple assaults, a robbery, and now a homicide to finish the day off.

Not that he hadn't had some crime-filled days on his beat before this, days when he thought that every hood in the city had picked his beat to ply his trade. There had also been days during his years on the force when he had been the unwilling observer of homicide victims, not to mention the countless times he had viewed the results of several other forms of the nightly mayhem that was practiced along the strip.

He would be the first to tell you that he had seen everything during his years on the force. But after today, he'd never be sure of that again. It seemed, he thought, that no matter how accustomed you became to death and violence, or to the sight of blood-soaked bodies, there was always a new and crueler way of dying that could surprise you enough to make your stomach churn and coil like snakes, and make you stick your head into a wilted potted plant in a hot hallway and heave your guts out.

The man was tightly bound with wire, seated in a wooden chair in a tiny kitchen. He was wearing black shoes and what had once been tan denim trousers. Now they were the rusty reddish black of dried blood. Above his waist he was bare, except for the T-shirt that had been twisted into a hard gag, jammed into his mouth, and tied behind his head.

Considering the surprising amount of blood that had

4

soaked into his trousers and collected into a sticky black pool under the chair, the man had taken a long time to die while somebody had peeled the skin from his chest in long, thin strips that still hung from his body like dried black strings. It was this surprising discovery that had caused Patrolman Packer to lose his lunch in the dead man's potted plant.

There were two patrol cars parked outside the building, their whirling lights flashing a red warning that this part of the neighborhood was an area to avoid. In this section of the city, cop cars did not attract crowds of eager onlookers hoping to witness some real-life drama. Here a patrol car could clear the street quicker than a winter blizzard or an approaching welfare worker.

In the apartment, two detectives from the River Station stood just inside the door while the patrolmen outside set up the unnecessary police barriers of white tape proclaiming PO-LICE LINE—DO NOT CROSS, which no one was the least interested in doing anyway. Tony Lonto was the older of the two detectives in the apartment. He was a tall and solid man with dark, no-nonsense eyes and black hair with a touch of gray at the temples. He had been a cop for more years than he liked to remember.

He had, in fact, been a cop for all of his adult life, and before that he had been a tough street kid who had finally decided that it was easier to be a cop than to be chased by one. He was now forty-one and he studied with guarded eyes the partly skinned man in the chair. Tony was accustomed to seeing death come in ugly ways, or perhaps after his years on the force he had learned to have very good control of his stomach. He inspected the apartment with care while he waited for the medical examiner and the lab crew to arrive at the grisly scene.

By any standards, it wasn't all that great an apartment. In this part of town a pimp or a pusher would likely have a better crib. In fact, even a second-rate burglar or an energetic mugger would have a finer apartment, on Silver Street, perhaps. This place looked as if it might have belonged to a working man who wasn't doing too well and who didn't have anything on the side for extra income.

Lonto decided that a second-floor, three-room walk-up on Terrance Avenue with a dirty window view of the street could not have been attractive to most burglars. And since the building also had some security, in the form of a double front entrance that required the residents to use their own keys, and a caretaker on duty, it would not be rated as a prime burglary target. But one look around the apartment was enough to convince him that someone had been searching desperately for something.

The contents of dresser and closet were scattered over the floor. A military-type duffel bag lay on the couch, which had been slashed open with a knife. The bag, too, had felt the sharp edge of steel cutting through it. A large green footlocker had been emptied and its cloth lining ripped out. It appeared that every drawer, box, chest, closet, and container in the apartment had been opened, torn apart, and examined in a very thorough and destructive search.

Lonto thought, from the apartment's appearance, that somebody had wanted something very badly. He glanced at the corpse again, then walked farther into the room so that he could look into the small bedroom. The bed had been stripped and the mattress slashed to ribbons. Okay, he thought, the place was gone over completely, not by a professional, perhaps, but it was done well enough so that it had taken some time to complete it.

He wondered what the poor bastard wired to the chair could have had that was worth what had been done to him. He also wondered about just how much courage, or whatever, it must have taken for the dead man to maintain his secret.

Lonto turned back to the living room when Runnion

opened the window and gulped in a deep and noisy breath of air. Detective Pat Runnion dressed as if he were on his way to a weekend ball game rather than working his shift as a police detective. He apparently had a theory that by wearing faded jeans and a loose, untucked shirt to cover the .38 clipped to his belt, he would blend in better with the street people whom he dealt with daily. Like, hey, fellas, I'm just one of the boys!

It didn't work.

Runnion could wear a priest's robes and he would still look like a cop. He was a big man, over six feet, with thick and curly hair which turned from brown to a straw-yellow in summer. He had hazel eyes and a wide, friendly smile. Yet he still looked like a big, mean street cop. In fact, to street people, he looked like a big, mean, two-hundred-twenty-pound cop who was two nightsticks wide in the shoulders, the type who would flash that big smile just before he pulled some cop's trick on you.

Having his dress-code theory repeatedly shot to hell every day did not seem to bother him much, but the fact was that he was a lot more comfortable in his jeans and loose shirts than he'd have been in a suit and tie.

He stood now at the window and wished that his stomach would stop acting as though it belonged to some green rookie fresh out of the academy. He cursed Patrolman Packer for not having had the decency to warn him and Lonto about what they would find in the apartment. He took out his handkerchief and mopped his sweating face.

"Jesus Christ," he said to Lonto. "I never saw anything like this crap before! What the hell happened to him?"

"Someone asked him a few questions," Lonto said, waving his hand over the room. "Whoever searched this place didn't find what they wanted and maybe figured they could persuade this guy to show it to them if they took off his skin."

"Nothing's worth that!" Runnion exclaimed, looking at the corpse. "Must have wanted something pretty bad, or hated this guy a lot to do that to him."

Lonto shook his head. "Who knows?" he said. "In this city you can get yourself killed for pocket change, so who knows what it takes to get yourself peeled."

"Did Packer find the guy?" Runnion asked.

"The super. He couldn't get an answer, so he let himself in, and then yelled for Packer on the beat."

"You know who he is yet?"

"Just the name on the door," Lonto said. He knelt by the ransacked dresser and studied something on the floor. "According to that, he's Walter Sullivan. Check his pockets for ID after the coroner and the lab people get here."

The coroner and the lab technicians arrived a few minutes later, and the apartment was suddenly crowded with busy men. You'd be surprised how many men one corpse can put to work. One body gets the attention of a coroner, a lab technician, a photographer, and one or two assistants, as well as the various policemen answering the call or learning the business of murder investigation. It is as if everyone wanted to get to know the person too late. Lonto and Runnion left them all with the corpse and called the super up into the hall.

He was a thin man in his late fifties, one of those sour-looking individuals who seem displeased with everything and find life in general to be a severe pain in the ass. He had thinning brown hair and pale blue eyes. His name was Lester Morkert.

"Tell me about this afternoon, Mr. Morkert," said Lonto.

"I already told the beat cop."

"I know," Lonto said patiently. "But let's go over the details. Do you know the dead man in there?"

"His name was Walter Sullivan. He's only been living here about three weeks."

"What time did you find the body?"

"About an hour ago. I found him and called the beat cop." He looked at his watch. "Must have been about five-thirty."

"How did it happen?"

"Well, I knocked first. I hadn't seen him all day, and I usually do. He goes out to eat at the diner every day like clockwork. Eight o'clock for breakfast and two o'clock for lunch. He didn't today, so I checked. I knocked and then used my key. That's how I found him."

"How did you know he wasn't out?" Runnion asked.

"Not him. He doesn't go out. Just to eat, three times a day, right on schedule. Any visiting or drinking he did, it was in his room."

"He have a lot of visitors?"

"Just one that I ever saw. He came pretty regular."

"How about today or last night?" Lonto asked. "Anybody around that didn't live in the building?"

"Not that I saw."

"Can you describe the man who visited Sullivan a lot?" Runnion asked, getting out his notebook.

Morkert thought about it. "Just an average guy, I guess. I only saw him in the hall once or twice."

"Tall? Short?"

Morkert shrugged. "Average, just a guy. Black hair, I think."

"Try to remember."

Morkert stared vacantly down the hall, then shrugged again.

"Okay," Lonto said. "You got worried about Mr. Sullivan not going out to eat as he usually did and decided to check on him. Is that right?"

"I wasn't worried," Morkert said flatly. "It was just unusual for him, so I checked."

9

"Hear any unusual noises up here either last night or to-day?" Runnion asked.

"Nope," Morkert responded. "Whatever happened in there was pretty quiet. He had that rag tied around his mouth anyway, didn't he?"

"It looks that way," Lonto said dryly.

"It scares a man," Morkert said. "Something like that happening to him in his own apartment." He thought about it for a moment and added, "I figured I shouldn't have rented to him from the start, you know? I just knew he'd be an extra problem, but not like this."

Lonto and Runnion looked at him in silence. Lonto broke the spell. "What made you think Sullivan would be an extra problem? He sounds like he was a good tenant."

Morkert glanced quickly at the apartment door, as though he thought Sullivan would hear him. "He was," he said hurriedly. "I just figured there would be extra problems in renting to a blind man."

Runnion sighed, and carefully closed his notebook. "Shit," he said.

"Thank you, Mr. Morkert," Lonto said. "We'll probably get back to you later."

"He really wasn't any extra problem," Morkert said as he walked toward the stairs.

The coroner was finished with Mr. Sullivan's grisly remains and met Lonto at the apartment door. "I'll get you a complete report with the autopsy, but I can give you some rough ideas right now."

Lonto waited for him to continue.

"Probably died late last night or mid-morning from any one of three things: acute shock, blood loss, or possibly his heart finally gave out. Anyway, he spent a long time in that chair, from the way his hands are swollen around the wire and the amount of bleeding he did. There's a lot of blood in there. It's my guess that whoever did it tied him up first and then searched the place, probably didn't find what they wanted until they started in on his chest."

He watched Lonto for a moment.

"That was probably when he was gagged. Looks to me like there's a pattern to the torture. One cut horizontally across the chest, just below the collarbone; then a series of vertical slashes about two inches apart from that top cut down to his waist," the coroner paused for a moment before finishing.

"Then, going from left to right, the skin was peeled down in two-inch strips. There's a pair of pliers in there, and a razor blade. I'd say the whole thing was done with those, but the guy probably died before they finished, since some of the strips haven't been peeled loose on the right side of his chest." The coroner shook his head. "You've got a real psycho this time, Tony. Whoever worked on this guy is plenty sick."

"Okay, thanks," Lonto said. "See if you can push the autopsy for us, Dave."

"Sure. I'll have the report over to you in the morning. That soon enough?"

"If the lab's done by then, it'll be fine." Lonto said.

Lonto remained in the doorway of the apartment and watched Detective Hooley, the police lab technician, and the coroner's two assistants systematically take the apartment apart in search of anything the police might find interesting or even, if they were really lucky, the reason why the apartment had been so thoroughly ransacked in the first place.

They took samples of everything in the room, including dust that they vacuumed up from the rug, the couch, and the dead man's clothing. They also bagged samples of spilled powders and liquids they found, and tagged them with neat cards for later identification. More often than not, such powders and fluids are later found to be not-very-exotic items, like face or foot powder or after-shave lotion. But the

11

police couldn't afford not to examine everything; one never knew what might turn out to be a very important clue. And, of course, after they had neatly cleaned up all of the spilled items they proceeded to make an even larger mess by dusting powder over the apartment in a search for fingerprints. It all looked very interesting and professional, if you were seeing it for the first time.

Lonto had seen it countless times, and was bored by the painstaking routine and deadening monotony of it all. Hooley looked around for the next place he wanted to dust for prints and looked at Lonto.

But since routine police procedure was at this point boring to him, his thoughts were on the man in the chair, or rather on another man had once seen in a similar condition. He did not like looking at this man, or thinking about the other man, because he could remember very clearly a North Korean village a long time ago, where some friendly ROK troops had wired a North Korean officer to an A-frame hay rack and then casually removed his skin in long strips.

They had not done it in order to extract any military secrets from him, but simply because he was North Korean and that was a standard treatment for any enemy unlucky enough to be captured by ROK troops. They had gone about the cruel task with a joking casualness that Lonto had found both frightening and sickening. He did not like finding a man who had died that way on Terrance Avenue. He did not like the thought of what sort of hatred was behind it or how valuable something was to merit that sort of viciousness. Just what the hell could a blind man possess to bring this on himself?

That was a good question. The public often felt that cops should be able to answer questions like it in a matter of hours, but Lonto knew that it wasn't going to work that way at all; it wouldn't be that easy. It was going to take a lot of routine work. Legwork and luck, he thought. The keys to finding any criminal, even a killer like the one who had butchered Sullivan. Luck might even be the more important of the two, unless whoever had committed the crime was just itching to get caught, but hardly anyone was itching in real life, just on television. Now there it seemed all of the crooks were itching to be arrested and have justice served by the end of the program. Unfortunately, there weren't any half-hour scripts to follow out on the real streets.

"Have you two finished?" the coroner's assistant asked. "We've got to take him out of here."

"How about it, Pat?" Lonto asked. "You seen enough?"

Runnion wiped his face as he answered. "I wish to hell I'd *never* seen this," he said. He looked pale, or what some laughingly call "green around the gills."

"Why don't you have another talk with the caretaker?" Lonto asked. "I'll finish up in here. I want to see what he's got in his pockets."

"Okay," Runnion said. "Maybe he'll remember something besides 'average' about Sullivan's visitor."

"I'd like to know a whole lot about that guy," Lonto said. "Maybe he'd be able to tell us how a blind man manages to get himself killed like this."

Detective Charles Hooley and the coroner's assistant had a long and busy night ahead of them, trying to find answers to the many questions concerning the dead man. There was, for example, the question of just exactly who he had been. It was all well and good to find a valid identification card in a man's pocket, complete with color photo, and to have another person, like the caretaker, say, "Yes, that is Walter B. Sullivan." But since the caretaker was not a relative, and this was a homicide case, the police ignored the available identification, wishing instead to rely on a check of the dead man's fingerprints. So they put aside the identification card, the brand new Veterans Administration Hospital outpatient card, and the social security card, and proceeded to identify the dead man the hard way.

Ask any police lab technician or assistant coroner—it is not at all easy to obtain fingerprints from a corpse, because you are definitely not going to get the desired cooperation from the subject. Instead, you have to ink each one of the eight fingers and two thumbs individually and roll the digits one by one into the proper space of each of four separate fingerprint cards. Then you have to ink the entire palm of each hand and take eight separate hand prints. That's a total of forty-eight separate prints. And if rigor mortis has set in, you have that further complication. Sometimes they were required to obtain the prints from a body in an advanced stage of decomposition, and the skin insisted upon falling off the fingers while the prints were being taken.

In the case of the man tentatively identified as Walter B. Sullivan, the only complications were incipient rigor mortis and the fact that his hands had been wired to the chair for several hours and were badly swollen.

This is a lot of work for nothing, Detective Hooley thought, after he had spent an hour and a half obtaining Sullivan's prints. I know goddamned well this guy is Walter B. Sullivan, just like his ID cards say. I know it, the VA Hospital knows it, and the Social Security Administration knows it. That should be enough. The trouble was, he decided, that the goddamned police department said they didn't know Walter B. Sullivan was Walter B. Sullivan! They probably thought Walter was Attila the Hun, or an international spy, and they wanted his fingerprints on file in case he committed any major crimes in the future, which wasn't likely, with Walter lying here still and a good part of his skin gone.

I should have been a bartender, Hooley thought, when he finished taking the forty-seventh print. Then I could listen to peoples' troubles rather than spend the night holding hands with old Walter here.

14

Hooley wondered why they were always doing things the hard way, especially since it was obvious that a blind man was not likely to be an international criminal or anything but a good citizen. After all, just how many illegal projects could a blind man be involved in?

They would send his prints off to Washington, the FBI, the Bureau of Criminal Identification, the city identification bureau, and, in this case, the Pentagon. And in a few days the BCI, FBI, city, or armed forces would notify the police that it was indeed Walter B. Sullivan's body tucked away in the morgue. Or they would notify them that they had absolutely no idea whose fingerprints were on the cards. In which case, Hooley knew, the police would decide that Walter B. Sullivan was a dandy name to finally type on all of these fingerprint cards.

It's a goddamned waste of time, Hooley thought again, as he completed the forty-eighth and last printing. And besides that, I'm going to get sick looking at this poor bastard, with his skin torn off his chest like somebody was going to use it to make lampshades. I would really like to be a bartender right now, Hooley thought again. Or maybe I should just stop looking at this guy and go on to the rest of the apartment. Hooley decided that was the best alternative.

2

The neighborhood had been through many changes during the years he'd been away.

Not that he had expected this part of the city to remain the same, really. He knew that the structure of the city would remain the same until the buildings fell down from age, but it was the people who transformed the neighborhoods as they moved in and overran them like warring armies moving back and forth across the city.

A neighborhood might be a mix of Irish, Italians, and blacks for several years, and slowly it would change to a Mexican one, or develop a Puerto Rican or Cuban flavor, and the storefronts would advertise their wares in Spanish. Foreign-sounding words on stores where once he had bought cigarettes. The buildings remain, he thought. The foreigners move in and everything changes on the surface, but it's still the same red-light district and the only type of life he knew.

He was back here to make his last big score, one that would pay him for his leg and for all the years of waiting for that bastard sergeant to get out of the hospital.

He had grown up in this neighborhood, one of the rank and file of a street gang calling themselves the Vice Lords. He had been a young man of twenty when a district judge gave him the choice of joining the army or going to the state prison for five years.

Prison would have been better than Vietnam had been, he knew now. Now, almost twenty years later, he knew that five years in Stoneridge would have been easier than the war, the loss of his leg, and the long years in the hospital. But if it all finally paid off now, it could be worth it. He could still put it all together and be on easy street for the rest of his life, if he could just figure out the sergeant's code before Shapiro got too impatient.

That lousy, stinking, iron-ass sergeant had just let himself die without saying a word. He didn't understand a guy like that. He'd known him for years and never really understood him, even when they'd decided to be partners over there.

Now what he had to do was let Shapiro know he was going to lie low for a while, until the heat died down. Give himself some time to work out that lousy code. But he'd better stay away from his apartment, too—just in case the cops came looking. So whom did he know who would put him up for a few days? The question was, whom could he trust? He sure as hell wasn't going to trust Shapiro and McCurdy!

Well, he could always find some strung-out hooker who would take care of him for a few days, as long as she got a taste of what he had to keep her happy.

Damn it, Sarge, I never meant for you to die, but you were always a stubborn bastard!

He went into a bar on the corner of Third and Washington. It was one of several rundown watering holes that Shapiro owned in the red-light district. Used to want to own a string of places like this himself, before he went to Nam;

used to think a lot about being a big man in the neighborhood during the nights, when those little yellow bastards weren't trying to kill him.

Sarge used to say that they were trying to kill everyone, not just him. But he'd always felt that every sonofabitch out there was shooting at him alone—even when Sarge had agreed to be his partner, and said he'd get him out of Nam alive if he did what he was told. He had always felt alone. Always alone. But Sarge had gotten him out alive, like he'd said. And now Sarge was dead, and here he was, alone again, alone with their big score.

The jukebox was playing a country-and-western number; whole damned neighborhood was either shit-kicker or Spanish music. You'd think this was Texas, or some other asshole place like it. The guy behind the bar was wearing a cowboy shirt, jeans, and a string tie. He was new, and Leo wondered where the regular bartender was today.

There were a couple of guys at a table in the back who he knew to be runners for Shapiro's numbers racket, and there was a young hooker at the bar. Baratto took a stool near the hooker and asked the bartender for a whiskey sour. The bartender seemed more interested in the shit-kicking music as he scowled and turned to the back bar and mixed the drink.

"Getting warm," Baratto said.

"What else is new?" the bartender asked.

"You new around here?"

"Why? You writing a book, or are you a cop?"

Baratto didn't think that was very funny. He stared at the man. "No," he said. "No book and no cop. But I'm not a smart-mouth bartender either."

"So, I'm new around here," the bartender said, and shrugged.

"My name's Leo Baratto, me and Shapiro go back a ways."

"You and the boss, huh?"

"That's right. We got a little business going."

"Baratto, huh?" The bartender shook his head. "Boss didn't say anything about you. You a partner or something?"

"Not exactly. We just have a sort of arrangement going."

"That's your business. You want to pay for the drink, please?"

"Just put it on my tab," Baratto said. "And while you're at it, give the lady over there a drink, too."

The bartender crossed his arms and shook his head. "Look, mister," he said. "I might be new, but I know that the boss don't run no booze tab for anyone. Now let's have a buck fifty."

Baratto pointed a finger at him, knowing that a new man would take some crap when he wasn't sure of his job. Baratto wanted the young hooker to see that he wasn't just some street cripple.

"Before you let that mouth get your ass fired, you'd better walk over to the cash register and look under the change drawer. You'll find that I do run a tab here."

The bartender hesitated a moment then went to the register and found the book on Baratto's bar charges. He quickly made Baratto another drink and served the hooker before he apologized to Baratto.

"Sorry about that, Mr. Baratto. No one told me you could have what you need on the cuff."

"Now you know," Baratto said. It felt good to know that he could walk into any of Shapiro's bars and get what he wanted. Shapiro's name lent him a sense of power, but he knew that Shapiro would expect his payback soon. He had carried Baratto and loaned him money for a long time now and was getting impatient for the deal he had been promised. Well, Baratto thought, I'll have to see that Shapiro doesn't get too impatient.

The young hooker slid off her stool and walked down the bar's length toward him. She was a tall and slender blonde, wearing tight red shorts and a red tube top. As she neared him, he could see the deep green of her eyes. She's a real looker, he thought. Then he noticed the tiny needle marks on the back of her hand as she raised her drink in salute.

Smart, he thought. Shoots her dope in her hand, where the marks could be from a scratch. But she's a junkie, all right. And for what he had in his pocket, she was going to provide him with a place to stay and some pussy too, if he wanted it.

He smiled at her as she sat down on the stool beside him.

On Wednesday morning, Detective Hooley called the Sixth Precinct and asked for Tony Lonto. He was very secretive and enormously pleased with himself. There was no question in his mind that he was indeed the Einstein of the police laboratory that morning. When Lonto got on the line, Hooley milked his information for all the suspense he could get.

"That murder on Terrance Avenue yesterday," he said. "I have the preliminary reports for you."

"Anything interesting?"

"Everything's interesting in this lab," Hooley said. "For instance, we have some dandy fingerprints that don't belong to the dead man."

"Fine."

"And they are the only prints in that apartment besides the dead man's," Hooley added. "We dusted everything."

"Fine," Lonto repeated. "Send them to BCI."

"I already did."

"What else?"

"I think we've got a motive for you," Hooley said in exultation.

Lonto waited. Then he finally said, "You want to let me in on it?"

"Well, you know we vacuumed the apartment?"

"Right."

"And we took samples of all items in the place."

"Right."

"We get a lot of very uninteresting things to test like that."

"Right."

"Like house dust and foot powder," Hooley said, enjoying himself. "Even crab powder. You'd be surprised by what we turn up at homicide scenes."

"So what did you find this time?"

"House dust and cigarette ashes," Hooley said. "Lots of that."

"Hooley," Lonto sighed. "Have you got something for me or are you going to screw around all morning?"

"Okay, okay," Hooley said. "What we've got is about two grams of ninety-nine-percent pure heroin. A nickel bag of this stuff, uncut, would OD any junky in town!"

"What?"

"Interesting, right?"

"Wait a minute," Lonto said, very interested now. "Where in the apartment did you pick that up? Do you remember?"

"We remember where all the samples come from," Hooley said officiously. "We bag and tag everything according to room and location. This stuff came from inside the duffel bag, which had a double bottom. You'll recall it was cut open."

"You sure the stuff is uncut?"

"This is pure horse," Hooley said, feeling superior. "I ran the tests three times. Nothing like it has ever come through here before! How's that for a motive? A blind man who's a pusher or bag man, and easy to rip off."

"It's a motive, all right."

"You don't like it?"

"Would you push dope if you were blind, Hooley? How the hell could he do it?"

"Well, there are lots of nuts in this city," Hooley said. "Maybe he liked to live dangerously."

Lonto decided that it really didn't matter whether the dead man had been a nut, or whether he had simply wanted to live dangerously, which was easy enough to do in the city. What did matter was that he was dead and that some very high-class heroin seemed to be involved. Those two facts were more than enough to send Lonto and Runnion back over to Terrance Avenue for another look at the murder scene.

In all truth, it was the sample of pure heroin that interested the cops very much. You'd think that cops who have been around long enough to be detectives would not be all that eager to respond to two grams of heroin. Not in a precinct where you could walk down Silver Street and bust fifty junkies and pushers on any given day for a total take of a couple pounds of various illegal drugs.

But the fact was that this particular two grams of heroin was rarer than a virgin on the strip. This particular two grams was definitely not street junk. This stuff, in fact, would scare the hell out of you if you were a cop who knew that street heroin was sold at a general purity of two to four percent, at best, and if you knew that when heroin came into the city at ninety-nine percent, it usually came in kilogram-sized batches right from a lab. And a kilo of that meant approximately sixty-four pounds of three-percent heroin to be sold on the streets. It was enough to give a cop a headache. An Excedrin-sized headache.

The caretaker at the Terrance Avenue apartment building was not overly pleased to see them. He was certain they had returned to make an even greater mess in the apartment than the one the lab technicians had left behind.

Lonto and Runnion let themselves into the apartment with the caretaker's key, and proceeded to make a *very* complete mess of the place. They did it one room at a time, and with the sort of determination usually reserved for professional wrecking crews. A burglar would have been pleased at their thoroughness. They began at ten in the morning, and they were still looking well into the afternoon. They had not found any more heroin in the apartment, pure or otherwise.

At four, they sat in the living room feeling like piano movers after a very long day. "Maybe the killer found it," Runnion said.

"If it was ever here," Lonto responded. "More than the two grams, anyway."

"Shit, Tony, you don't sew just that little bit of smack into a duffel bag. There had to be more."

"Did we miss any place he could've stashed it?" Lonto asked.

Both men unconsciously looked around the room, shaking their heads in a silent and negative response to Lonto's question.

"So whatever was here is going to turn up on the streets," Lonto said. "Maybe we'll get a lead on it then."

"Sure. How do you figure this, Tony? A blind guy getting killed like that. That's really strange, and then this smack in addition. It just doesn't add up that he could be a pusher or bag man. It's not exactly a blind man's vocation."

Lonto sighed. "Look, Pat," he said. "I've seen pushers who were in wheelchairs, and one who was an eighty-two-year-old grandmother. Anybody can be a pusher. If that's what this guy was, then he's simply the first *blind* one we've run into."

"Know what I think?"

"What?"

"That maybe if we find out something about this guy, things will add up some."

"Probably will," Lonto said. "And we'll start that little project by checking the place he ate his meals at. And then we're going to check everything about him, all the way back to the day he was born."

"Tonight?" Runnion asked, alarmed.

Lonto grinned. "No. This evening we just check the place where he ate. Then I'm going home."

"Date?"

"Well, Robin's flight gets in later this afternoon, and she's got a two-day layover here. Is that a date?"

Runnion grinned. "Sounds like time enough for an orgy."

"Sure," Lonto said. "So let's go see where this guy ate. Maybe we'll learn something."

Al's Sandwich Shop, on the corner of Grant and Terrance, was an excellent place for a blind man to eat. It would improve the entire meal if you could not see the cockroaches and flies that populated the place, or the overflowing garbage cans visible through the open door leading back into the kitchen. The owner, who doubled as cook, was named George Jenkins, and when Lonto and Runnion arrived, he was seated at an empty counter, drinking a cup of coffee. The detectives bravely ordered coffee and joined him.

"Yeah, I know Sullivan," he said. "You think I get so many customers in here I wouldn't remember a blind man? He's been coming in here about a month or so."

"He came in regularly, then?"

"Ate all of his meals here," Jenkins said. "I usually seen him two, three times a day."

"When did you last see him?"

"Let's see, this is Wednesday, right? I guess Monday morning he was in here. Had bacon, eggs, and hash browns, like usual. I ain't seen him since then."

"Anybody with him Monday?"

"He came in alone. Most of the time he'd be alone."

"How about before Monday, was there anyone in here with him then?"

"You mean that smart sonofabitch that came in with him a couple of times, right?" Jenkins asked. "I wouldn't forget that bastard."

"Who?"

"Sullivan called him Lee or maybe Leo. Something like that."

"Can you describe this guy?" Runnion asked, hopefully.

"Who forgets an asshole like that?" Jenkins exclaimed. He pointed to Lonto. "Looks something like you, sort of dark. Like he had some wop or spick in him. About your size, too. Only he was greasy-looking, like he didn't wash much. Real bum."

"Seen him around here much?"

"Naw. He started coming in about the time Sullivan did. What do you want him for?"

"Just some questions we want to ask him."

"Would you give us a call at the Sixth Precinct if he comes in here again?"

"Damned right! What'd he do?"

"He might know something about Sullivan's murder."

"So that's who got killed down the street, huh?" Jenkins said. "I seen the meat wagon down there the other night. He was a good customer."

"Did Sullivan and this other guy ever do anything unusual in here?" Lonto asked. "Argue or anything?"

"The creep *always* argued with Sullivan," Jenkins said. "Sullivan would sit there and eat and the creep would argue. Got pretty loud sometimes."

"Did he threaten Sullivan?"

"I never heard him. I don't pay that much attention to what the customers are saying. I just told him to shut up when he got real loud. He threw a coffee cup at me just for that."

"Anything else?" Lonto asked.

"You guys shouldn't have much trouble finding him."

"What makes you say that?"

"Hell," Jenkins said, "just look for a mean little bastard with a bum leg!"

"A what?"

"A bum leg. Something was wrong with his right leg," Jenkins said. "He limped."

Lonto and Runnion agreed that it was a good item to end their workday on. At least they had more now than they began with, and everything helped.

Tony Lonto did not go to his apartment after signing out at the precinct; instead, he went to an apartment in Highland Park Heights on Central Avenue.

It was his first chance in six days to see Robin Hall, and he had visions of a long evening in her bed. He had been thinking of Robin on and off throughout the day. In fact, she had been on his mind most of the past week. To tell the truth, he was somewhat hurt and upset that Robin had chosen to move out of his apartment and into one of her own, a high-priced place in an exclusive suburb. She said her reason was that the place was closer to the airport and her job there as a flight attendant.

To Lonto the reasons for her move were clear and resulted from a problem in their relationship—two problems, in fact. He wouldn't change his feeling that cops, or at least some cops, like him, should not marry. He was uncomfortable with the thought of asking a woman to share his life, a life that could quite likely end in a sudden and violent fashion, and well before his retirement rolled around.

The other thing that distanced him from Robin was the difference in their ages. At twenty-seven, Robin saw no problem in Lonto's forty-one years. Lonto saw it as a problem; he loved her completely and in every way, but he felt she both needed and deserved more from life than being the wife of a middle-aged cop, a type of person seen by Lonto as an endangered species.

She greeted him at her door with hugs and kisses accompanied by eager sounds of delight.

"Wow!" Tony exclaimed. "Am I to take it by this display that you missed me some?"

"Every day and night!"

She led him into the apartment, kissed him on the cheek, and said, "Fix us a drink, will you?"

"You want a seven-seven?"

Robin stretched and sat on the couch with her legs folded under her. "That's fine, hon."

"How was the flight?" Tony asked while he was mixing their drinks.

"Very routine. The usual sore feet and a couple of pinch marks on my butt. I think I'm getting tired of it, Tony. Eight years flying is enough. I love it, but there has to be something else. Something a girl can spend a lifetime at."

"You're qualified," Lonto said. "You wouldn't have any problem finding something in the city."

"What is wrong with you, Tony? I don't want a lifetime job in some office. I don't want to be a 'career woman.'"

"You just said—"

"I said I wanted something to spend my life doing. Something every woman wants. I told you all this before I moved out of your place and asked you to think about us, just before I left on this last flight."

"I know you did, hon."

"Then why are you acting stupid? I want a home and I want to have a baby, our baby. You're just acting like this to upset me."

"I don't want to upset you, Robin. I'm not trying to. I just thought we had talked all this out before."

"Did you think about it while I was away?"

"Some," Lonto sighed. "The problems are still there."

"*Your* problems," Robin said. "I don't have any problems with being with you and sharing your life."

27

"But, Robin . . ."

"Don't 'but, Robin' me, damn it! You think I'm not able to make my own decisions, that I don't realize there are problems in being married to a cop? I can make my own choices, Tony. Stop trying to protect me from a cruel world!"

"Robin, I love you. I love everything about you!"

"Then make me your wife and let me take my chances with you."

"Robin, hon, can't we keep what we have and leave things alone? Then maybe you'll find something you really want later and still be free to take it."

"I know what I want, damn you!" she exclaimed. "You don't love me. I'll bet you didn't even miss me!"

"I love you and I miss you like crazy every day that we're apart. I miss you at my place, too."

"You just miss my being there to make love!"

"Of course I do," Lonto said. "What's wrong with that? I miss your being there, period. I miss everything about you, your love, your warmth, and your company."

"You don't think I know my own mind," Robin said. "You want to protect me from life, hide me from it."

"Jesus, Robin, I do not!"

"Then let me make my own mistakes in life. Let me decide what's best for me. Don't patronize me."

"Hon, it's just that—"

"That you're trying to say what's best for me. I don't have any say in my own life, right?" She sniffed. "You won't even listen. You just prattle on with your chauvinism."

"Maybe I'd better go home, Robin."

"Of course! Leave me alone. I haven't seen you in six days and you want to leave."

"Robin . . ."

"Just because I love you and want to have your children is no reason to stay. Just because I know my own mind isn't any reason. Just go ahead, leave! You didn't miss me!"

"Jesus!" Lonto said in exasperation.

"Sure, Jesus. Blame it on anyone but yourself."

"Come here," Lonto said, watching her and thinking how much he loved her and how empty his life had been before they met.

"I know what you're thinking," Robin said. "That won't solve anything."

"It's a start," Tony said. "We could talk some. You did say that you missed me too, didn't you?"

"I know your talk," Robin said, moving over to his side and putting her arms around his neck. "I missed you like crazy, Tony."

He kissed her gently. "I missed you, too. A lot. We can talk about it later. Pillow talk."

She smiled and held him close. "Just about us. Just hold me close and we'll talk about us later."

Lonto held her, tightly, silently.

About the time that Lonto and Robin were settling down for a quiet evening at home, Julian Shapiro was preparing for his evening's work in the red-light district.

Early in his career, an evening's work for Big Julie had ranged from muggings to numbers running to dope pushing to pimping for a few of the neighborhood girls whom he had convinced that it made more sense to sell what they were giving away. It made sense for the girls to avoid getting slapped around by Big Julie. As Big Julie had moved up in the rackets, he had graduated to work like loansharking, enforcing, bookmaking, and running a string of massage parlors and out-call services for higher-priced hookers. By that time he had picked up a few loyal partners, like Frank McCurdy, who was street-wise enough to know that while he had the muscle to succeed on the street, he didn't have the intelligence necessary to run an operation the size and scope of Big Julie's. Frank was also smart enough to realize that when Shapiro moved up in the rackets, someone usually had a fatal accident to make room for him. On the streets it is always best to offer your services and loyalty to someone who makes your future secure along with his own.

Big Julie Shapiro was now secure in his position in the city's rackets. He had carved out his comfortable empire from the red-light district, where he ran his girls, dope, numbers, bookmaking and loansharking. He also owned bars, flophouses, hotels, massage parlors, and call-girl services. He knew what he needed to invest in order to make more money and expand his kingdom.

Over the years the people on the street had learned that Shapiro was a lot like the weather; you could bitch about him, but you had to live with him.

Shapiro enjoyed starting his working day by taking a cruise around his empire, just to remind his subjects who it was that they were required to keep happy in order to continue conducting their businesses. It wasn't that he received a percentage of every racket or crime in his kingdom; indeed, he allowed for a certain amount of what he liked to think of as free enterprise. After all, everyone has to make a living. But the things that were his remained his alone. He maintained his empire by dispensing rather convincing object lessons to anyone violating his rules or coming up short during his collections.

In the red-light district, between Silver Street on the river side and Terrance Avenue to the west, the "businessmen" were sometimes confronted with the problem of not having enough money for booze, drugs, women, food, and the rent, as well as for paying off Shapiro. But that was no real problem; if Shapiro wasn't paid, his goon McCurdy hospitalized you, and there you'd get no drugs, booze, or women anyway. And the county took care of your rent, if you lived.

On this particular evening, McCurdy was imparting an object lesson to a bookie in an alley off Silver Street, while Shapiro coolly watched his enforcer practice his art. Mc-

Curdy was busy beating the Puerto Rican man to a pulp. McCurdy was a six-foot-four-inch mean sonofabitch. With the face of an ex-pug who had taken a few too many punches and his two hundred fifty pounds, none of which was fat, McCurdy would have made it big in professional wrestling.

The Puerto Rican bookie, new to the city, had made the mistake of trying to skim some cash off the top of the weekend baseball betting proceeds. McCurdy had dragged him from a bar on Shapiro's orders and had then drop-kicked him into the alley next to the bar, where he could be worked on in private. McCurdy had then broken both of the man's arms—just to make sure, he informed Shapiro, that "the little spick don't pull no blade on me." Now McCurdy was beating the man bloody with his hamlike fists. Shapiro watched and offered an occasional suggestion. McCurdy ended the lesson by stomping the bookie into the alley's grime with his size-twelve shoes. He then relieved the bookie of his wallet, passing it to Shapiro.

Though Shapiro had not joined in brutalizing the little Hispanic, nobody doubted the depths of his deadliness. Shapiro, too, was over six feet; and though he was well-muscled, there was an overlay of fat that lent him a Buddha-like appearance, somewhat benevolent if you could ignore his mean eyes.

He had always been overweight, bordering on obesity, and his size often gave opponents the illusion of slowness on his part. This erroneous assumption was seldom made twice since Shapiro had a trigger-quick temper, and a razor-sharp butterfly knife secured in a wrist sheath. The knife could drop instantly into his waiting hand and a flick of his wrist would snap open the six-inch blade, resulting in severe damage to an antagonist.

Many had witnessed ugly scenes of slashed throats pumping blood onto the ground, of an eye hanging by a thread on a cheek covered with gushing crimson. Nobody wished to get on Shapiro's shit-list, as had the unfortunate bookie.

31

McCurdy wiped his hands on a handkerchief while Shapiro counted the money from the wallet. "All there, boss?"

"About seven hundred and change," Shapiro said. He tucked the money into his jacket pocket, kicked the unconscious bookie in the head, and strode out of the alley, McCurdy following a step behind him.

Shapiro paused for a moment on the sidewalk to contemplate his next move. He decided that while he was on Pimp's Row, as the street was known colloquially, he might as well make his collections from the prostitutes and then take the car back to his headquarters.

There were four blocks on Silver Street that were called John's Walk—in addition to Pimp's Row. The locals used the former while the police used the latter. In either instance it was the area where one could get anything from a twenty-dollar blow job to a five-hundred-dollar call girl, as well as odds-on chances of contracting one of a number of venereal diseases to take home to the little woman.

Shapiro had put most of the girls in bars and massage parlors and ran an out-call, dial-a-lady service with the youngest and most attractive females he controlled. There was nothing in the line of sex that one couldn't buy from Shapiro's operatives. After spending a profitable hour making collection stops, Shapiro and his right-hand man made their last stop at a hookers' hangout called Topless Harry's. Harry's was crowded with working girls and sweating customers. On Pimp's Row every night was party time, so long as the customers had money in their hands. There were girls for every taste and preference, white, black, brown, and Asian, and each was skilled in the arts of romance. Every whim was obtainable, from back-booth quickies to trios spending a long night together, any kind of trio.

Shapiro and McCurdy took their usual place at a booth reserved for them in the back and were swiftly served by the owner, who curried Shapiro's favor in an effort to stay in business and retain the major portion of his earnings, minus Shapiro's cut, of course.

McCurdy leaned across toward the man and asked, "Has Baratto called in the last day or so?"

"No," the owner responded. "Nobody's seen him around, either. You heard anything?"

"Only that he's making himself hard to find," McCurdy answered.

"That little prick's into me for a few grand already," Shapiro said. "He better not be trying to pull any shit!"

"You figure he did the job, then?" McCurdy asked.

"Sure, he did it. From what I heard, his old partner had half the skin cut off him."

"Then," McCurdy whispered, leaning closer to Shapiro, "Baratto's got the stuff."

"Either that or he knows where it is."

"Then why hasn't he called?"

"Could be he wants to let the heat die down."

"Maybe he just wants to dig the stuff up and skip town," McCurdy observed. "He can sell that stuff anywhere."

Shapiro let his eyes roam the room. A few tables away, a very young blond girl was seated with an older redhead who had her hand inside a john's fly. The blonde looked about fifteen, and nervous. Shapiro smiled to himself.

"He's not going anywhere with that stuff," Shapiro said, dragging his eyes away from the blonde. "He's not that smart. What would a punk like him do with a couple of million dollars worth of grade-A stuff? He'll bring it to me."

"I don't trust him."

Shapiro smiled. "I don't either, that's why we put the word out tonight that I want him and that it's worth a few C-notes to whoever finds him. Maybe it's time we paid him a call at his girlfriend's place. He might be there."

McCurdy grinned in anticipation. He had never liked Baratto.

Thursday began as a lousy day with no promise of improvement. August had always been a lousy month of stifling heat, and this August was a scorcher. There had not been a cloud over the city in three weeks, just a fiercely blue sky and the heat, undistrubed by even a hint of a breeze.

According to police statistics, the month of August has the second highest crime rate of the year, December coming in first, what with every hood in town doing his Christmas shoplifting and pocket-picking in the holiday crowds. But August was second. It seemed that the long, hot days brought all the city's crazies out. And the heat made tempers short all around town.

At five-thirty that morning, a bank teller living in the St. Frances Park area decided to mow his lawn before breakfast, having been unable to sleep well in the sticky humidity of his bedroom. His neighbor, and Friday-night cribbage partner, resented having his sleep interrupted on this bright day, and he made his displeasure known to his neighbor with his son's baseball bat. When the police arrived they found the bank teller quite dead beside his lawn mower while his neighbor stood above him, the bloodstained bat in his hand. It was what the cops call an open-and-shut case.

What Lonto and Runnion had was definitely *not* an open-and-shut case, however. At nine that morning Detective Charles Hooley called from the lab to give Lonto additional information he had received from the state Bureau of Criminal Identification. The BCI was strictly a collection unit for information on statewide criminal activities and movement. Just as each precinct had its own files on known offenders within their jurisdiction, the state kept a larger collection of information on its native sons and daughters who had come to the attention of the authorities. And since any and all persons charged with a crime within the state were fingerprinted and photographed, the files of the bureau were extensive, and their active listings went back at least ten years.

Hooley's request for I&I, identification and information, was answered from those files in the city and from the army and the FBI. When Hooley reached Lonto he got right down to the business at hand.

"The dead man on Terrance Avenue has been positively identified as Walter B. Sullivan. It came in this morning from the feds, along with his military record."

"Any priors?"

"Nope," Hooley responded. "Not even a traffic ticket. But that figures. His service record goes back fourteen years and he had been an inpatient at the Veterans Hospital in Apple Grove for the last seven years. He was discharged less than a month ago. It's the other guy who's got the record."

"What other guy?" Lonto demanded.

"The other prints from Sullivan's apartment belong to Leo Baratto. He's a local boy with a record for assault. BCI identified him. I'll send both packages to you."

"Is there a current address for Baratto?"

"Yeah," Hooley answered. "But I doubt if it's any good. According to this record, some judge gave Baratto a choice about nine years ago, enlist or do time."

"And he enlisted?"

"That's what it says here. Anyway, I'll send this stuff over right away. I just wanted to let you know it was in and on the way, and to give you a message."

"What is it?"

"You're supposed to call the coroner at your earliest convenience."

"Okay, thanks, Hooley."

"You know what I think?"

"What?" Lonto asked, not wanting to know.

"Baratto's your killer."

"You think that's possible, huh?"

"Don't you?"

"I think it's the worst case of suicide I've ever seen," Lonto said. "How about that?"

"Smartass!" Hooley said, and hung up.

Lonto grinned to himself as he put down the phone. He then filled Pat Runnion in on the latest information as they left the station house. Lonto was wearing a tan suit and Runnion his usual combination of jeans and a shirt. Both men moved with brisk sureness, and despite their difference in attire they left one with the impression that they were a team.

They drove across town in silence and on into the suburbs. They relaxed in the heat and enjoyed the view of the city outside the slum areas in which they generally spent their working hours. Sometimes it was difficult to remember that the entire city was not all one big red-light district and den of iniquity, or simply block after block of garbage-filled alleys and decaying buildings. Sometimes one forgot that there were residential areas with beautiful homes and green lawns alive with children, places in the city where there wasn't a pimp or pusher for miles. And when one did remember, and saw the good places in the city, one was reminded of why being a cop was both important and positive. Both men enjoyed their morning ride and said nothing about the case during their journey.

The Apple Grove Veterans Hospital was located in a residential area on River Road. It was two blocks above the river, with a wide, tree-filled lawn surrounding it. The hospital itself was a modern, six-story building of glass and stone, with an air of spaciousness and freedom about it. Despite the open cheerfulness of the grounds and the brisk newness of the place, there was no doubt in a visitor's mind that it was indeed a hospital, with the same depressing atmosphere usually found in any place associated with the business of disease and death. This particular hospital was perhaps even

36

more involved with death than other hospitals simply because its rooms and wards were crowded with the damaged bodies and minds from three wars. It was a place where men waited to die; for years they lay in wait. Distant wars had given them no choice, and all of the victory parades were equally distant memories, bitter memories. These men had not marched to the cheers of crowds, but had crept onto these grounds in the bellies of ambulances.

Since it was both a large hospital and a military facility, this ensured a great deal of red tape for the curious to combat. A badge did not guarantee anything in these surroundings; it could only serve to open doors, it did not assure entry. A cop was simply another inquiring outsider, to be shunted, sidetracked, and delayed until someone in authority made a decision to satisfy a visitor's curiosity by providing answers and information, or inflame it by declining to do so.

After forty-five minutes of waiting, Lonto and Runnion found themselves in a well-furnished outer office, facing a tough-looking captain in the Medical Corps who seemed better suited to leading troops in the field than to the medical insignia he wore on his collar. The impression one received from him was that one had better have a damned good reason to be in that office. The captain was tall and solid, wore a crewcut, and had eyes that made you think you were back in boot camp on day one of your hitch.

"Good morning, Captain. I'm Detective Lonto and this is my partner, Detective Runnion. We're investigating the murder of a former patient of this hospital, Walter Sullivan. We have been informed that he was here until the tenth of July."

"So I've heard," the captain said. "My name is Bob Taylor, I'm a staff doctor." He stood to shake their hands, and then gestured to two chairs in front of his desk as he sank into his own, drawing a manila folder from his desk drawer as he settled down.

"A murder, huh? How did it happen?"

"We're investigating to find that out, Doctor," Lonto replied. "So far we have a name and this hospital to begin with. Was he in fact a patient here?"

Taylor opened the file in front of him. "Sullivan, Walter B., sergeant, infantry. White, age forty-two, six-foot-one, weight one-ninety-seven. Blinded in Vietnam. Sound like your man?"

"The FBI identified him through his service records, Doctor. That certainly matches what we've gotten so far."

"Then how can we help you here?"

"Just how long was Sullivan a patient here?"

"Close to six years. He transferred from Walter Reed Hospital."

"Isn't that a rather lengthy hospitalization, even for a blind man?" Lonto asked.

"Of course. If it was just his loss of sight, we'd have had him functioning in society within two years," Taylor said. "Unfortunately, in Sullivan's case there were several major complications and operations before we could be sure he would be anything more than a vegetable. Head wounds and damage to the motor nerves are very touchy."

"Were you his physician?"

"I was never formally assigned to his case," Taylor replied. "But he, or his type of case at least, was really well known around the hospital."

"How so?"

"He was a fighter, he fought every inch of the way and made himself recover," Taylor said. "Some of the men we receive here just lie down and die, no matter what we do. But Sullivan was one who decided to live at any cost and against any odds, and did it. He had recovered enough by last July to be placed on outpatient status."

"Then he could function as well as any blind man can in society?" Lonto asked.

"Not quite." Taylor paused. "He had developed his senses and skills as well as he could. In all the training he undertook, such as braille reading and self-maintenance, he did very well—better than average, in fact. But because of his head wounds it was necessary that he be careful physically with himself. It wouldn't have been possible for him to lead a very active life."

"A blind man wouldn't have a very active life."

"A blind man, the usual blind man, Detective, doesn't have to live with shell fragments in his head," Taylor said. "Sullivan knew that those fragments could kill him at any moment. He insisted on leaving the hospital despite that knowledge."

"Sounds like a determined man," Runnion observed.

"Very much so," Taylor replied.

"Does the hospital keep any records on who visited him?" Lonto asked.

Taylor shook his head. "No, we don't do that."

"Is there anybody who might know who visited Sullivan?" Runnion asked.

"Possibly his ward nurse, someone who saw him daily. You can ask around," Taylor said.

"Any trouble between him and other patients?" Lonto asked.

"Not that I'm aware of."

"Would you say he got along well with the staff here?"

"I think so, yes. Our staff is quite professional."

"Did he fool around with any of the nurses, date any?" Runnion inquired.

"I have no idea what his relationships with the nurses might have been. He was not, as I indicated, my patient. I suppose he might have, however."

"What?"

"Dated the nurses. Most of our long-time patients do. The nurses' station on his floor can give you information concerning his personal activities."

"Do you know," Lonto probed, "if he was a junky?"

"What?"

"An addict. Was he addicted to drugs that you know of, or is there anything in his files to indicate he might have been? I mean, a lot of guys coming out of Nam had that problem."

Taylor reopened the file and read through it quickly. He seemed impatient. "There's nothing in here that indicates addiction," he stated. "The usual medications were prescribed, but there's nothing out of the ordinary. He was given a prescription for pain relief when he left us."

"What was it?" Lonto asked.

"Let's see." Taylor paused. "It was a thirty-day oral Demerol prescription. He renewed it once."

"Is heroin used medically in this hospital, Doctor?" Lonto inquired.

"Not in any form," Taylor said, shaking his head. "It's not a drug a doctor can or would give a patient. We have better drugs than that, anyway. Was Sullivan involved in drugs?"

"We're not sure," Lonto replied.

"I wonder if you'd check on something for us, Doctor," Runnion said. "Could you tell us if a Leo Baratto has ever been a patient here?"

"Is he a serviceman?"

"Yes. At least he was. Would you check that out?"

Taylor shrugged and reached for the phone and dialed the records department. "This is Doctor Taylor. Will you go into the files and see if we've had a Leo Baratto as a patient? If so, please bring his file to my office as soon as you find it. Thank you." He hung up. "It will take a few minutes."

"What did you think of Sullivan, Doctor?" Lonto asked him. "Did you like him?"

40

"Personally?"

"Yes."

"We didn't have that sort of a relationship," Taylor said, and paused. "I didn't really get to know the man, even on a doctor-patient basis. This administrative work keeps me out of the wards for the most part. But Sullivan was a topic of conversation in the doctors' lounge. As I said, the man fought valiantly for years to get well, and I believe every doctor in this hospital knew about him. We like to see our men get well enough to leave here, and you have to admire a man who strives as hard as Sullivan did."

"Why do you suppose he wanted to get out of here so badly?" Lonto asked. "I understood his home was in Montana."

"He has a sister there, I believe—according to this file," Taylor said. "I really couldn't say why he wanted to live in the city." A knock at the door interrupted Taylor. It was opened by a young blond woman about twenty years of age who walked briskly to Taylor's desk and handed a file to the doctor, smiled at him, and then winked broadly at both detectives as she walked back to the door and out of the office.

"That," Taylor explained, "was Linda." He glanced at the file. "And this is the file of Leo Baratto."

Lonto and Runnion waited expectantly as Taylor began to read quickly through the file.

"Can we have his description?" Runnion asked.

"White male, black hair, brown eyes, five feet eleven inches tall, weight one hundred ninety pounds. He was a patient here three years ago and is on outpatient status now."

"Do you have an address for him?" Lonto asked.

"Yes, but it's three years old. It's Eight-three-six-oh East Cedar Avenue," Taylor said.

"Can you tell us when he was last here?"

"Let's see. The last appointment he kept was on July second. He didn't show up for this month's appointment. Actually, judging by his chart, he's only kept about one out of every four appointments since his outpatient status began. Just enough to keep his disability pay and have his prosthetic adjusted a few times.''

"Prosthetic?" Runnion blurted.

"He lost his right leg below the knee in Nam. He was with us for that and psychiatric treatment.''

"Do you know if he was a friend of Sullivan's?''

"I have no idea. Let's see, their respective wards were located on opposite ends of the hospital, but of course it is possible. Why not ask him?''

"We will," Lonto promised. "Just as soon as we find him.'' He paused a moment. "There is one other thing you can help us with, Doctor.''

"And that is?''

"The nurses who might have known Sullivan. Could you assure them that they won't be penalized for talking to us? Your staff is not at all talkative.''

Taylor grinned. "It's policy, patient information is privileged. But in this case I'll call the charge nurse. It's station fifty-one on the third floor.''

Lonto and Runnion thanked him for his time and help and started to leave the office when Taylor stopped them. "One thing you might like to ask Mr. Baratto when you see him is what outfit he served with in Nam.''

They waited.

"Both he and Sullivan were in the First Battle Group of the Eighth Infantry. It's a big outfit, but they could have known each other over there; they were wounded about the same time. Perhaps they were in the same company or platoon, even.''

Lonto grinned his thanks. "We'll certainly do that, Doctor Taylor. Thanks again.''

They spent over an hour questioning those nurses who had known Sullivan, and at the end of that time they decided that they had gathered all of the information they were likely to obtain from the hospital personnel. One item they picked up was that Sullivan had indeed been dating a nurse on a regular basis for the past two years. Her name was Pamela Eling. She was not on duty that day.

Both men were content with what they had gathered. A nurse who knew both Sullivan and Baratto informed the two detectives that those men had indeed known one another; they had not only served in Vietnam together, but had been wounded on the same combat patrol and sent back to the States together. According to the nurse, it appeared that the relationship between the two men was a classic example of opposites attracting, so unalike were they, at least on the surface.

Sullivan was the career soldier type, down to the tips of his spit-shined boots; Baratto was stockade-bait, out of trouble only when his unit was in direct contact with the enemy. It made little sense to Lonto that a man from the Montana ranch country would have anything to do with a small-time, big-city street punk like Baratto. Not even a war zone should have been able to pull those two together into a close relationship. They had seemed to spend much of their time together arguing, but they had always returned to each other's company. Lonto wondered what the tie was that bound them together.

Perhaps Lonto had been a cop too long to buy the "old war buddy" routine; perhaps he had arrested too many lifelong friends, people who were friends because of business, dope, money, or a criminal partnership. The friendships usually ended abruptly when the business failed or the money, the dope, or the partnership began to crumble from one cause or another.

To Lonto, the Sullivan-Baratto friendship was pure bullshit. He wanted very much to know why he felt as he did, and he expected Leo Baratto to supply an answer to that question also. Now all they had to do was find Baratto and ask him those questions, and they hoped they knew exactly where to start looking for him.

3

The young hooker Baratto had picked up in the bar had an apartment about six blocks away. She told Baratto that her name was Nicki and that she was from Iowa, but had been born in Houston, Texas, which explained the soft drawl she spoke with. She told every john that she was just a corn-fed country girl who was trying to get by in the big city as best she could. For some reason the johns seemed to enjoy shoving it to a poor country girl trapped into sin by the harsh realities of urban life.

In truth, however, she had started selling her body when she was thirteen, for extra school money, and had enjoyed it. Hooking was an easy way to pay for the extras her family couldn't afford. And before she had quit her educational pursuits in order to devote more time to the world's oldest profession, she had been introduced into the world of drugs. A bit of speed and marijuana at first, then downers, and finally the never-never land of heroin and cocaine. It had been her Houston pusher who had given her the first hit of smack, and she had stayed with him when he drove north to find a bigger and better supplier in this city. She had promptly left him when his supplies ran out and he was picked up for trying to rob another pusher who turned out to be an undercover cop.

Nicki's real name was Thelma Higgins, but she felt that "Nicki" had more class and glamour for a girl who figured to make it big in the art of separating men from their money with a few minutes work on her back—or whatever position the johns desired. She had good looks, a fine, hard body, and a vulnerable expression that made the johns want to help her, usually with a large tip added to the fee she charged.

Shortly after her arrival in the city, she had begun to work the streets, and soon she had learned that when you worked johns on Pimp's Row you'd better make damned sure Shapiro received his cut. In return, she was permitted to work the bars and massage parlors and was provided with some regular clients who called her as they desired her services. But a girl had to work, and she didn't need to give Shapiro any part of her tips, so she made out very nicely. She figured that after another year or so she'd have enough put aside to allow her to move to a smaller city and open her own place, perhaps a bar, maybe a massage parlor. The first words she said to Baratto when she sat beside him at the bar were, "You look lonely, mister, and I'm the best company you'll find around here."

Baratto had agreed that he could use some company, and before they had finished their third drink he had maneuvered his finger far enough up the leg of her tight shorts to know that she wasn't wearing any panties. He was feeling the booze, but was sober enough to know that the girl was maybe seventeen or eighteen, and if the heat was on so that you wanted to get off the streets for a few days, then a good young hooker wasn't a bad choice to spend those days with. He put his hand on the girl's crotch and asked, "You got a place near here?"

"You want to have a party, huh?"

"Yeah," he replied. "Just you and me and some white magic I've got in my pocket."

"Okay, honey," she said. "If you've got some good stuff, I'll give you a party you'll never forget. Let's get out of here."

"Sure," Baratto said. He waved casually at the bartender as they rose to leave, and Nicki noticed that he had run a tab and knew that anybody who could run a tab in one of Shapiro's places should also have a good dope connection. Never mind that the guy had a bad leg and limped, she'd screw a basket if there was some really good dope involved. She figured that if she played her hand right she could keep this joker well-screwed and herself high for a few days. She hooked her arm through Baratto's as they moved toward the exit.

By the time they reached Nicki's small apartment, Baratto's leg was aching. When they had first fitted him for the leg, the doctors had told him the pain would decrease as he became used to the prosthetic and as the leg itself adjusted to its new attachment. Decrease, my ass! Baratto mumbled to himself.

At times the leg ached when he had the attachment off. It felt as if his foot was there and killing him, even while it lay rotting on the other side of the planet. Still, he grudgingly admitted to himself, I suppose I'm better off than a lot of the guys, the ones who lost both legs, for instance. Or that guy from Philly who lost his nuts. Yeah, he thought, I'd rather have my balls than a foot, especially tonight, with this broad.

He also compared himself to the blind Sarge. I could never have made it blind, Baratto thought. Never. Sarge dealt with it. The tough bastard really handled it. But in the city you had to be more than tough, you had to be smart, too.

"You live here alone?" he asked Nicki.

"Sure, you don't think I've got kids, do you?"

"Why not? Some of the girls around have kids at fourteen, fifteen," he said. "By the way, what's this going to cost me?"

"Depends on what you want," she replied, squeezing his hand. "We can talk about it inside."

The apartment was a small efficiency on the second floor. It had one window that looked out on an alley. Next to the window was a fan noisily moving warm air from one part of the room to another, providing no relief in the process. The place was clean, and Baratto was surprised to see a large teddy bear perched on the pillow at the head of the bed. He pulled close the curtains at the bedroom door and walked to the couch, where he sat, motioning Nicki to do the same. She sat next to him.

"Is Nicki your real name?"

"Sure. What's yours?"

"Leo. Leo Baratto," he said. "Nice Swedish name, huh?"

"Swedish?" she repeated. "Yeah, like spaghetti is Irish."

"So, what do you figure this is going to cost me?"

"How about a C-note?"

"In Nam we bought pussy for five bucks a night," he said. "You think I'm some rich john from uptown?"

"This," she replied, "is the good ol' U.S. of A., where everything costs more."

"Hell, I can get laid in any massage parlor for forty bucks, and you know it!"

"How about fifty?"

"How about twenty to take care of the overhead, and I'll give you a couple of good hits of some pure China white?"

"Okay," she said quickly. She was smiling. She would have screwed him for nothing, if he had good heroin. "But let's get high first, okay? Then we can screw all you want."

"Sure," he said. He took a plastic bag from his pocket. The bag was half-filled with white powder. "This is right out of the poppy-field labs in Asia, baby. Pure, uncut shit. Pure white dreams. You got a fit here?"

"In the dresser," she said. She always kept a syringe handy. She had a steady craving for heroin, especially when she was working. She brought to the table in front of the couch the syringe, water, a spoon, and a candle, and watched with eager eyes as Baratto prepared the first shot.

"You'll like this kid," he promised. "This is the stuff that junkies dream of copping. The stuff they sell on the street is maybe five percent. They cut it with all sorts of crap. With this you can only use about a match-head dose or it will OD you fast. How long you been using, anyway?"

"About a year," she replied. "Not steady, though, just once or twice a week. Why?"

"You think I want to risk knocking you out with a hit of this? That would be like fucking a sack of flour."

"Don't worry about it, daddy. You take care of me and you'll get all the pussy you can handle, or anything else you want."

"You a three-way girl?" he asked, grinning.

"Honey, I'll take it any way you want to give it to me," she declared. "Is that ready yet?" She was thinking about the heroin and what he had told her about its potency. She was wondering if she would be able to talk him into giving her a nice piece of it. If it was as pure as he'd said, then he was holding thousands of dollars worth in that bag, more than enough to keep her high for months.

She hadn't liked the way he seemed to know a lot

about dope and the streets. He was not just some dumb john out to get his rocks off. She suspected he might be a pusher for Shapiro. In that case, the only way in which she could get some of the heroin was to keep him happy. But that was okay, screwing was almost nice when she was high.

"Here it is, kid," he said, handing her the syringe. "You want me to do it for you?"

"No. I can do it."

He watched her, with a smile on his face, as she carefully shot the drug into a vein on the back of her hand. Her eyes closed slowly and a loose smile crossed her face. In a moment, it seemed, she had passed into ecstasy.

"Good, huh?" he asked.

"Good? No. Beautiful!" she exclaimed. "Man, that's fantastic!" She stood and stretched lazily, then slowly pulled her sweater over her head and dropped it to the floor. "Aren't you going to take a hit?" she asked him.

"Not yet," he said. "One hit of that stuff and I wouldn't be able to get up the energy to fuck." He pulled her down onto his lap and cupped one of her breasts. "Nice tits."

"You like them?"

"I like everything you got," he said. "Let's see what you can do with all this nice equipment you have."

She showed him.

Half of the customers she had brought to her place had some sort of weird sexual request or preference. Baratto had part of a leg missing, but his sexual appetite was fairly standard. Most of her other customers would brag that they were going to fuck her for hours, and run out of gas in fifteen minutes. Not that she minded. It was her business to get them off, up, and out in good time. But none of those other customers had come with a bag of heroin. She gave Baratto everything he desired and joined him in another hit of heroin.

By morning she had agreed with Baratto that he should stay there with her for a few days. He could, she thought, stay as long as his heroin lasted. She had already managed to pinch several hits from the bag while he was in the bathroom, and had it safely hidden. If she could keep him around, she could get more.

Around ten in the morning she got a call from the service she worked for, and turned to him when she hung up the phone. "Listen," she said, "if you don't mind, I have to go out for a while."

"Customer?" Leo asked from the bed.

"Yeah, a regular. You don't mind?"

"Hell, go ahead—you can't wear it out."

"You're going to stay until I get back?"

"I'll be here. You got anything to eat?"

"I'll fix us something nice when I get back," she said. "I'll only be gone about an hour."

"No rush," he said. "I'm not going anyplace today. Besides, there's a few things we haven't tried yet."

"I doubt that," she said, winking. "But I'll hurry back." She left the apartment and headed for the stairs.

He lay on the bed, his hands behind his head, and stared up at the ceiling. She'd be back as soon as she could, he knew. He had everything she wanted right in his pocket. He could keep her, he knew, as long as he took care of her habit. She would do anything he wanted. And what he wanted was to lie low for a few days and plan his leavetaking. He could always find a woman, once he had the rest of the heroin.

After a few minutes he got up and took a worn Bible from his jacket and began to study it carefully. He had to figure out the damned code. He knew time was against him. Shapiro would soon be hunting for him, and since he hadn't shared the score with Sarge, he sure as hell wasn't going to deal with Shapiro, either! Sarge, at least, had earned his share, he thought. Now it's all mine.

The code has to be here, he thought.

The building at 8360 East Cedar Avenue was a brownstone in the middle of a block in the old Walker's Bluff section of the city. Once, when the river traffic was the city's lifeblood, living in Walker's Bluff had been a key to the city's high-society circles. It was a status symbol to live there and look out over the river and the red-light district from a high and safe perch. The years had brought the slums to Walker's Bluff, right onto the safe and lofty perch. The only status symbols the cops found there now were an occasional pimp-mobile and a nattily dressed numbers collector making his rounds of the now-shabby brownstones.

This particular building still held vague hints of yester-day's elegance. Carved stonework and walnut inlays spoke of past wealth. The wino snoring on the stoop told of today's poverty. The kids playing stickball in the street watched si-lently as Lonto and Runnion entered the foyer of the build-ing and began scanning the mailboxes.

Leo Baratto was listed in apartment 2B.

The building held years of slum decay inside with the heat. There was no fresh air or light on the stairwell, only the choking smell of urine, decomposing garbage, and age. A musty, damp odor of rotting wood was an added ingredient that almost drove the two cops back outdoors.

As they reached the second-floor landing they disturbed the lunch of a huge rat that stood on its hind legs and glared at them. It had been feeding on the soggy remains of a Big Mac. The bag the burger had come in was ripped to shreds, the burger sitting in the middle of the remains of the bag as if the rat were using it for a plate. The two cops looked at the rat and then at each other. Silently they walked along the wall, leaving about three feet between themselves and the animal.

Turning down the hall toward 2B, Runnion looked back

at the rat. "That motherfucker looks like a young panther," he said to Lonto.

"Yeah, I wish I'd brought a nightstick! I'd have beat that Big Mac right out his ass."

Apartment 2B was the second on the right at the beginning of the hall. Lonto drew his revolver and listened at the door while Runnion, gun drawn, braced himself against the wall opposite the apartment door. On TV, cops smash down doors with their shoulders; those doors are balsa wood, made to fall apart. On the real streets, the average door would crush a shoulder. The foot was the key. It is much more practical, especially in these old buildings, except, of course, when street-smart dope pushers have reinforced the door with steel bars of plating. This is guaranteed to fracture a leg. It also gives the occupants extra time to escape through a back door or window.

At Lonto's signal and with a great deal of prior experience backing up his two hundred pounds, Runnion kicked the door with a flat foot just under the latch. The lock sprang and took out a good-sized chunk of the doorjamb. The door crashed back into the wall as the two cops swiftly entered the apartment. They came in crouched, guns out in front and eyes darting over the room. Lonto almost fired on a gray cat that was scrambling to get out of a broken windowpane. They froze in the silence, carefully looking over the room, then moving into the others. Except for the departed cat, the apartment had been empty.

"See if you can find the super, Pat. I'll start up here."

"Okay," Runnion replied. "You know, if that fucking cat could shoot like he can run, we'd both be dead!"

"Yeah, fast sonofabitch, wasn't he?" Lonto said.

Baratto's apartment was contributing its full share to the accumulated stench pervading the building's atmosphere. It was small and cluttered and there was a coat of grime on the walls and other surfaces. The sort of filth that is born of neglect. The rooms were ripe with the sour odor of sweat, urine, and rotting food. It reminded Lonto of the odor in the monkey house at the zoo.

There were newspapers, magazines, and dirty clothing scattered around and, among them, thirty-seven empty booze bottles. In the kitchen, the sink was full of food-caked dishes and utensils, and the table was covered with half-eaten TV dinners. That was apparently where the cat had been feasting, probably as an alternative to fighting that rat. In the heat and clutter, there was no chance of judging accurately how long the dinners had been sitting there.

The only room that gave any indication of periodic cleaning was the bathroom, where the sink and shower stall hinted at occasional use. A man's shaving gear rested in the medicine cabinet and a well-used bar of soap was in the shower. A pile of dirty and dingy shorts and T-shirts lay beside the toilet, and there were three dirty towels on the shower-curtain rod.

The bedroom held a more careless clutter of soiled clothes and a bed covered with stained and graying sheets. The apartment did have other occupants, Lonto now noted. Hordes of cockroaches scurried about in every room, oblivious of his presence. He realized that with his absence from the kitchen table area the roaches had attacked the TV dinners en masse. The sights and smells drove Lonto to the window, which he forced open as wide as it would go. He stuck his head out and discovered that the everyday odors that had assaulted his senses upon leaving the car now seemed somewhat more fragrant in comparison with the apartment's stench.

After a minute he returned to his inspection, going to the one closet in the bedroom. In the tight little space was more dirty clothing and an army duffel bag with Baratto's name and serial number stenciled on it. Inside the bag, Lonto found letters and military-related papers along with several batches of photos of soldiers in combat dress and gear.

The bedroom dresser produced several sets of new underclothing, an address book, and a well-cared-for army .45-caliber automatic. Lonto was looking through the the bottom drawer of the dresser when Runnion appeared with another man.

"This is Mr. Dupaloff," Runnion said. "He's the super."

"I'm Detective Lonto, Mr. Dupaloff. We'd like to ask you some questions."

Dupaloff scratched his balding head and watched them uneasily.

"There's nothing I can tell you about anything," Dupaloff said. "I mind my own business."

"All we need is some information concerning the occupant of this apartment."

"I already said I don't know nothing about him."

"Mr. Dupaloff, it is too goddamned hot and smelly in here for us to waste time. I want to get out of here as fast as possible. So either you talk to me now or we can go downtown and talk in an air-conditioned room. It's your choice, make it now!"

"You think I got nothing to do but talk to cops? What do you want to know, anyway? I got things to take care of around here!"

"I'm sure you're a busy man," Lonto said. "But we'll keep it short. Who lives in this apartment?"

"Leo Baratto pays the rent on it. He's not here a lot."

"Has he been here long?"

"I guess about, oh, two, two and a half years."

"Anyone share this place with him?"

"Would you?" Dupaloff laughed. "He ain't here much, but when he is, he's alone."

"About how much time does he spend here?"

Dupaloff shrugged. "Not a lot. He gets a government

check every month and lives with some cunt somewhere, I guess."

"Make a guess."

"He's in and out! Hell, I don't keep track as long as the rent's paid."

"Do you know who he stays with when he's not here?"

"He never said and I don't ask. I mean, we ain't real close friends or nothing like that."

"When did you last see him?"

"Who knows? I'd say about a week ago."

"Would it have been this past weekend?"

"I was drunk then, I didn't see nobody."

"Listen, Tony," Runnion interjected, "I think we should take this guy downtown." He turned to Dupaloff. "You ever been in jail, Dupaloff?"

"Well, certainly, I been in jail. Been in the drunk tank."

"I don't think that's necessary yet, Pat," Lonto said. "Mr. Dupaloff, you can save us all some time and trouble if you'd just try to remember."

"Why you guys want Baratto?"

"He's a suspect in a murder case," Runnion said coldly. "That's why he's wanted, that's why what we ask you is important, and that's why we want answers!"

"Who'd he kill? That cunt he shacks with, I bet!"

"What makes you say that?" Lonto asked.

"That's the only place I know of where he goes to."

"How about recalling when you last saw him." Runnion suggested.

Dupaloff shrugged. "Well, I guess it was this past weekend. Saturday, maybe."

"How long did he stay?" Runnion asked.

"I don't know if he did. If it was Saturday, I only saw him going out. I was by my window."

"Drinking?" Lonto asked.

"I was working at it."

55

"But you're sure you did see him?" Lonto asked.

"I thought it was him."

"Was he alone?" Runnion asked.

"He's always alone."

"What did he do when he left the building?" Runnion asked.

"Like he always does, went down to the corner and waited for a bus."

"Which bus?" Lonto asked.

"Hell, I don't know."

"Did Baratto ever mention owning a car?" Runnion asked.

"I never heard and never saw him drive one. Only time I saw him in a car was when his cunt dropped him off."

"Did you get a look at her?" Lonto asked.

"Not much of one."

"Describe her for us?" Lonto suggested.

"Just a young tramp. Black hair, I think."

"Good looking?" Lonto asked.

"Good enough to get his government check, I guess!"

"How old was she?" Runnion asked.

"Hell, ask Baratto. She's his shack-up piece, not mine. Younger than he is, that's for sure!"

"How old is Baratto?" Runnion asked. "Do you know that?"

"Forty or so," Dupaloff said. "She wasn't with him for his age or his wooden leg, that's for sure."

"Describe him," Lonto said.

"Sort of stocky, with black hair, dark eyes, and a phony leg, like I said."

"Anything else? Scars? Beard? Mustache?" Lonto asked.

"Nope."

"How'd he talk?" Runnion asked.

"Like we do. He wasn't any refugee, you know."

"I mean soft, gruff, deep?" Runnion said.

"He talked like anybody around here. Knew all the street talk."

"Did Baratto eat or work around here?" Lonto asked.

"I don't know," Dupaloff said. "I mind my own business as long as the rent's paid on time."

Lonto closed his notebook. He was used to asking questions and not getting many answers from citizens who always simply wanted to mind their own business. That usually meant that where a cop was concerned, they were deaf, dumb, and blind, but actually minded everyone's business. He didn't like it, but he'd grown up in the same streets himself and he understood. He nodded at the caretaker.

"That's about it for now, Mr. Dupaloff," he said. "If you recall anything else, or if Baratto shows up here, I want you to call us immediately."

"I ain't going to remember nothing," Dupaloff said. "I done told you what I know." He looked at them with suspicion in his eyes. "There going to be cops all over this place now?" he asked.

"My partner and I will be here for a while yet. Then some of our lab people will be here to check the place over. After that, an officer will be in this apartment in case Baratto returns," Lonto told him.

"That's what I meant! Cops all over the place. You guys done with me?"

Lonto nodded. "Thank you, Mr. Dupaloff."

They watched him leave the apartment, then looked at each other and then around the room.

"Shit," Runnion exclaimed. "I think I'll go get us some rubber gloves before we shake this place down."

"Let's call Hooley and get at it," Lonto said. "I don't want to spend any more time than I have to here."

Sometimes you get lucky on a case and all sorts of interesting information turns up in return for very little work. Cops need a little good fortune now and then, too. Lonto and Runnion searched the apartment for two hours before Hooley finally arrived, and by then they knew where they were going next. They also felt that enough evidence had been gathered to link Sullivan's murder to drugs. Leo Baratto's apartment had produced some interesting items.

Item: Between four and five grams of heroin found inside the base of the telephone. It didn't take much imagination to guess that the heroin would probably test out to be as pure as that found in Sullivan's place.

Item: An army-issue Colt .45 semiautomatic that, being the suspicious characters they were, they assumed was both unlicensed and likely stolen.

Item: A photo of a group of soldiers with the caption "Fire Team Alpha" written across the front of the photo and a list of names identifying the pictured people on the back. The soldiers were identified as Sergeant Walter Sullivan, Corporal Arlen Nimlos, Corporal Derek Kinder, PFC Asa Arcum, PFC Albert Beall, Private Virgil Staffer, and Private Leo Baratto.

There were no doubts in the minds of the detectives that Sullivan and Baratto had known one another very well. And finally, from an address book in the dresser they extracted the name and address of Baratto's girlfriend, one Cheryl Rand, who lived at 4250 Eighth Avenue North.

The address was itself interesting. They were sure that Ms. Rand was, as the super had tactfully described her, "Baratto's shack-up." Moreover, the address was right where they would find him. They left Hooley busily dusting the apartment and went to find out how right they were.

Cheryl Rand's address was in one of the newer apartment complexes in the city's old business district. It had a doorman who didn't like policemen and was not in the least impressed by detectives. He stopped Lonto and Runnion in the lobby and called for the landlady to come and deal with them.

The landlady didn't like policemen either, and she particularly didn't like cops who just might be vice squad detectives. Her dislike possibly stemmed from her experiences in paying off or being busted by various vice cops when she had worked the streets as a hooker. But it was more likely that her still-smoldering dislike was fed by fear, considering that eight of the twenty units in the complex were occupied by ladies whose income was either gained from or supplemented by turning tricks in their apartments.

A percentage of that income always worked its way into the landlady's bank account. So the landlady thought that the two detectives were there either to cut in on the operation or to bust it up. Neither prospect made her very happy, and she thought it a damned shame that the cops wouldn't let her and her tenants simply go their way, minding their own business. Her displeasure and fear combined to make her tell Lonto that there was no damned need for any cops to be prowling around and bothering her tenants, hardworking people trying to get by, and why couldn't the police just leave decent people alone.

Lonto, who knew damned well what some of the ladies in the building did for a living, patiently explained that they were there only to talk with Cheryl Rand about a friend of hers, a friend suspected of murder. Lonto went on to advise her that it would be in her best interest, and that of her tenants, if she were to cooperate in full, and that if she didn't he would instead talk to her now about all of the male visitors coming and going at the complex, as reported by the beat officer.

The landlady said she didn't know what he was talking about but that she recognized her duty to provide the police force with assistance in the fight against crime, being a law-abiding citizen and one who didn't want killers running around loose. Accordingly, she produced a key and handed it to Lonto, who advised her not to phone the Rand apartment and to wait in her own apartment until he and Runnion returned. Runnion pointed at the doorman and told him not to leave the lobby and also to make no phone calls.

They took the elevator to the fourth floor and found the Rand apartment at the end of the hall. While Lonto gently eased the key into the lock, Runnion stood to the side and pressed his ear to the door. Both men had their guns in hand. He heard nothing except the muted tones of a soap opera.

What Runnion wanted to hear was a conversation or laughter from living people. That would tell him the occupants were involved with one another and unsuspecting of imminent visitors with guns and badges. And if they were unsuspecting, then they were not waiting, guns in hand, for two cops to enter. Runnion stood there listening for approximately five minutes. He whispered to Lonto, "I don't hear anything but the television." He then moved to the side of the door opposite Lonto.

Both men tensed and took deep breaths as Lonto turned the key slowly. When the door was unlocked, Lonto, just as slowly, turned the doorknob, and when the door was open both men followed its swing into the room. Runnion went to the right and Lonto to the left, both crouching, guns extended at arm's length. There was no hail of lead to greet them. Except for the television, only silence welcomed them.

They began moving through the apartment with precision teamwork, quick, sure, and ready for any eventuality. They learned quickly that there was nothing living in the apartment.

They found the dead girl on the bathroom floor.

There was nothing exciting or messy about her death, no knife or gunshot wounds or any sign of violence or blood, just a very dead and cold body laying on a pale blue rug and clad only in a pair of bikini panties. At first glance she looked asleep. There was a syringe lying on the rug beside her, and several burnt matches. In the sink was a spoon and a wad of cotton. It would be easy, if also obvious, to assume she'd died of an overdose, the kind of death that claimed junkies on a daily basis, nationwide. Another addict who'd found the cure to addiction, a blissful journey to whatever awaited them on "the other side."

Disregarding first impressions, however obvious and commanding they might be, Lonto and Runnion treated this discovery exactly as they would have treated an ax-murder victim, because all unexplained deaths are assumed to be murders until the facts dictate a different conclusion. They called the case in and notified the coroner's office, the police laboratory, and their commanding officer. They also brought the landlady upstairs to identify the body.

"Yes," she told them, "that's Cheryl Rand in there."

The dead girl was a blonde. She had been tall, with a slim figure and long legs. She was a very attractive girl, the kind you see winning beauty contests or being chosen homecoming queen.

"You are sure this is Cheryl Rand?" Lonto asked.

"Of course I'm sure," the landlady stated. "Her roommate has dark hair."

They were standing in the living room, waiting for the coroner and lab technicians to arrive.

"I know all the girls who live here. Cheryl and Colleen share this apartment."

"What's her roommate's full name?" Lonto asked.

"Colleen Emerson."

"How long have they lived here together?"

"They rented the place together from the beginning, about six, seven months ago," the landlady replied. "They were two good residents, paid their rent on time and never caused any problems."

No problems, Lonto thought. Well, she doesn't have any

now, but we do! He had the sudden cold belief that there was now a certainty of a large amount of pure heroin loose in the city. Junkies are usually quite sure of the dosage of heroin they need to get high but not dead. If a user was given pure heroin and fixed the same amount he or she was accustomed to when using normally cut street smack, an OD was a foregone conclusion.

It was police instinct that convinced Lonto that a major disaster was about to befall the city. They hadn't many facts to go on, no hard information from the network of informants both men had built up over the years, not even the usual whispers preceding the arrival of a new supply of drugs. Lonto wasn't worried about the lack of hard evidence, but he was concerned by the lack of input from informants, knowing as he did that roughly eighty-five percent of cases are built upon the information provided police by stoolies. It was from that information that hard evidence and facts ultimately emerged.

His instincts were spurred by the available facts: two murders, both tied to heroin and both linked to Leo Baratto, in whose apartment heroin had been found. It is out there, Lonto thought. A time bomb ticking slowly. He was about to begin questioning the landlady again when a movement in the hall and the turning of a key in the apartment door froze him.

He moved to the side of the door, pulling the landlady with him, and forced her into a crouch behind him as he drew his weapon. As the door opened, Lonto grabbed it and forced it fully open while aiming the gun and shouting "Freeze!"

A pretty, dark-haired woman stood in the doorway with a look of wide-eyed fright on her face; it passed quickly as she assumed the offensive. "What the hell is this?" she demanded to know.

"Just hold it right there," Lonto ordered, surprised at the

appearance of this very attractive woman, and her poise. She was tall and slender, with curving hips, dark auburn hair, and a nice tan. All of the very pleasant features stopped at the hard look in her eyes and the firm set of clenched jaws.

"Is this your apartment?" Lonto asked.

"That's Colleen Emerson," the landlady interjected.

"Yes, this is my apartment. Who the hell are you, and why are you in my apartment?"

Lonto showed her his shield and asked if she knew a Leo Baratto.

"What is this?" she replied. "Sure, I know him. Cheryl and he are together a lot. Where's Cheryl anyway? And what's going on here?"

"You'd better have a seat," Lonto said. He guided her to the couch and waited while Runnion escorted the landlady from the apartment and then returned.

"When did you last see Cheryl Rand?" Lonto asked.

"She was here when I left," Colleen answered. "Is she in trouble?"

"Was anyone here with her when you left?"

She looked from one to the other and said, "She was alone."

"Was she expecting anyone?"

Since she had sat down and arranged herself in a comfortable position, Lonto was able to observe the needle marks under the tan of her arms and hands. The marks explained why the two women had lived together and why they knew Baratto, who was probably their supplier. Lonto also decided that Colleen wasn't worried enough yet to answer questions in the manner he desired. He sat next to her and turned to face her, speaking to Runnion as he looked the girl in the eye.

"Take her in there and see if she can identify her junky friend, Pat."

He watched Runnion lead her to the bathroom door,

noted her surprise at seeing the body, and observed the change in her eyes and walk when Runnion led her back to the couch. She wasn't playing her "average city girl" act now, she was back to being Colleen Emerson, addict, who was a high-priced hooker to support her habit, and one who was experienced with cops.

The hard, calculating look in her eyes said she knew she had problems and was wondering what she had to give up to get rid of them. The cops she knew usually wanted a piece of the action or a piece of her. She sensed that this time, however, free samples and money would be insufficient to help her.

Lonto, still watching her, waiting for the appropriate moment to begin questioning her, had seen the look and the mental gymnastics before and understood what was now happening in the girl's head. It wasn't an easy situation for her, he knew, especially since she was a junky. If she didn't cooperate, she could end up downtown in a cell, unexpectedly and unwillingly kicking her habit cold turkey, and losing her list of clients at the same time. The johns she serviced would look elsewhere for the same sex and companionship she provided. And they would find it.

If, on the other hand, she gave up too much to the police, that information might very well filter back to the streets and she would be tagged as a stool pigeon, which would make it impossible for her to find a pusher who would sell to her and would scare off both her johns and her friends. It could also lead to her death.

Lonto and the woman shared a silent understanding of her dilemma, and both knew they would have to play their respective roles correctly, each of them trying to get from the other more than they surrendered in the exchange.

Lonto spoke first. "What is the name of your junky friend in there? Is that Cheryl Rand?"

"Yes, that's Cheryl," Colleen replied. "Look, I don't want any trouble."

"Lady, trouble you've already got," Runnion advised her. "This is your apartment and you are the last person to have been, by your own words, alone with the deceased."

"How long have you been out of the apartment?" Lonto asked.

"About four, five hours," she said, looking at her watch.

"When did you leave here?"

"Oh, about nine this morning."

"Where did you go?"

"Just out, you know."

"No, tell me. Out where?"

"I had an appointment. A guy."

"Where?"

"Hill Crest Motel, on Highway Eight."

"What was this guy's name?"

"I didn't ask."

"Well, then, it isn't very likely he'll be able to verify your story, is it?" Runnion asked her.

"He was just a trick, but they'll remember me at the motel."

"What time did you get there?"

"Our appointment was for one o'clock."

"Where were you before that?"

"I had breakfast and had my hair done, and, before you ask, I ate at that restaurant next to Henri's salon in the Brook Wood Mall."

"We'll check, you know. Are you sure of your facts?"

"Go ahead and check! I'm not going to lie. I wasn't here and I don't want any trouble."

"Why didn't you have the john come here? Don't you turn tricks here, like Cheryl did with Baratto?"

"I told you, Leo and Cheryl had an arrangement. I don't cut in on her action, and vice versa. She was waiting for somebody here, so I had to meet my trick somewhere else. I've used that motel before."

"How long had she been seeing Baratto?"

Colleen shrugged. "Since we moved in here. Not regular at first. She'd just see him once or twice a month. Probably all he could afford. Lately she's been seeing a lot of him."

"Was he the one she was waiting for today?"

"I don't know. She only said she had an appointment. I would guess maybe it wasn't him because she said 'an appointment,' not 'Leo.'"

"Baratto was a paying customer?"

"More or less."

"Either he's a paying customer or he isn't. Which is it?"

"They had an arrangement."

"Tell us about it."

"He'd come around whenever he got the urge," she said. "He sent a few customers over, too."

"Was he pimping for the two of you?"

"He'd just steer a few guys our way. Cheryl slept with him when he wanted to. It wasn't any kind of real pimping thing, more or less friendly, you know? He knew a few guys who'd pay, he'd send them here."

"How old was Cheryl?"

"Twenty-two, I think."

"Baratto's in his forties, isn't he?"

"Yeah, I guess. Most of our tricks are older guys," Colleen said. "Maybe Cheryl liked older men. Anyway, she said he had some big deal coming up and she wanted him around when it came through."

"What sort of deal?"

"Just a deal."

"But you don't think it was Baratto she was waiting for today?"

She shook her head. "I don't think so. Like I said, she just said an appointment—and I've been here when Leo came over. I think she was expecting somebody she wanted to see alone. Besides, Baratto never made appointments, he'd just come over."

"How well did you know him?"

"Baratto? We made it a few times. He'd come around, and if Cheryl was out, he and I would get it on."

"Was he a paying customer of yours, or did you have an arrangement with him, too?"

"Look," Colleen bristled. "So I'm a junky and Baratto had some real good stuff, but that's better than buying it from some pusher on the street."

"Baratto is your supplier, then?"

"No, not regular. He didn't sell to us. Just when he wanted to get laid he'd bring some stuff with him. He got laid and we got high. As far as I know, that was his arrangement with Cheryl, too."

"He wasn't a regular customer, then?"

Colleen shook her head. "I don't think he was pushing," she said. "He would only supply us with some when he was in the mood to get balled. Like he was bringing some of his private stock."

"Did Baratto ever give Cheryl an extra piece, keep her supplied?"

"I don't know. If so, she never shared any of it with me."

"Where did Baratto get his heroin?" Lonto asked her.

"Jesus, I don't know! He knows a lot of street people. He was always bragging about that big deal he was expecting, a deal with Big Julie."

"Who?" Runnion demanded.

"Julian Shapiro," Lonto interjected. "You know him. He and his pet dinosaur, Trunk McCurdy, run most of the dirty business in the area." He turned back to the girl.

"Is Shapiro Leo's connection?"

"I told you I don't know where he cops from, just that he always talked about his big deal. I don't ask any questions about Shapiro, anyway."

"Did Baratto ever talk about any of his friends from his army days?"

"You mean the guy he called Sarge?" Colleen asked. "He talked about him a lot, like they were real tight."

"What was Sarge's name?"

"Sully, I think. Yeah, Sully. He never came here, but Leo has been waiting for him to get out of some hospital ever since Leo started coming over here."

"Was the name Walter Sullivan?"

"I'm not sure I ever heard that." She paused. "But I think Leo used the name 'Wally' once or twice. He was also in on the big deal Leo talked about having with Shapiro."

"But Leo never said exactly what kind of deal it was, is that right?" Lonto asked.

"All Leo ever said was that when he and his buddy were ready, they were going to be rich. He said they were already rich, all they needed to do was get together on the streets. But I never saw Leo with any money to throw around."

"Let's get back to when you left here today," Lonto said. "Did Cheryl say anything at all to indicate who she was waiting for?"

"Just that it was a real important appointment," Colleen answered. "She wanted to meet whoever it was alone, almost chased me out."

"Miss, you were lucky," Runnion observed.

"Huh?"

"There'd be two corpses in there if you'd stayed."

"Do you have any idea where Baratto might be?" Lonto asked her.

"He might be at his friend Sully's place."

"Sullivan's dead," Lonto told her. "Any other places, bars he hung out in, favorite clubs?"

"Nothing that I know of. He could be anywhere, for all I knew about him. Look, you guys, I don't want any trouble over this, okay? I've told you everything I know, but don't let Leo know that I talked to you about him, okay?"

The detectives sat silently watching her as she made her plea.

Colleen sighed and crossed her long legs. "You're not going to bust me, are you?" she asked. "I could like, uh, take care of you guys if you want, anything you want."

"Forget it," Lonto barked at her. "We have to take you down to the station."

"You're going to bust me?"

"We need your full statement, typed and signed by you," Lonto told her. "If everything checks out, you'll be back here this evening."

"It will check out," Colleen assured them. "I wasn't even here." She smiled at them and added, "I wouldn't mind if you guys did come over sometime, you know?"

They grinned at her.

"I'm really quite good." She grinned back.

Some people are not hampered by the kinds of legalities and restrictions that policemen work under in their search for people. The police meet many obstacles: reluctant witnesses, people who will never give a cop the time of day, some who want a lawyer present even though they are not suspects and are simply being asked for information, and, of course, all those who say they don't want to get involved.

The police need search warrants, court orders, and three yards of red tape and a book fat with rules and departmental regulations governing every facet of police work. It is not easy for policemen to do their job.

Two people who were not hampered by such rules and regulations were Shapiro and McCurdy. They had their own rules and methods for locating people in whom they were interested.

They had paid a visit to Baratto's girlfriend, and had vacated her apartment not too long before Lonto and Runnion had arrived. She had been most cooperative about giving them Baratto's whereabouts, especially when McCurdy had given her a nice shot of heroin and Shapiro had promised her a good-sized supply of it for her own. He had balanced his offer with another promise, to make her life very short and terrible if she didn't divulge every fact she held. Shapiro felt that she had indeed been very helpful before she died.

In addition to giving them Baratto's address, she had also allowed them to partake of her charms before she prepared to sample her first and last shot of the deadly potion McCurdy had handed her in fulfillment of Shapiro's promise. But it was not until they had arrived at Baratto's apartment that they realized Cheryl Rand's information was outdated and useless. Baratto's apartment had been sealed by the police, their sticker warnings pasted on the door. As an alternative, Shapiro knocked on the door of the caretaker, Mr. Dupaloff.

In this particular section of the city, a knock on one's door usually presaged trouble of some sort. This was no exception for Mr. Dupaloff. In times past, people had come to his door to tell him that his wife had run off with a local pimp, that the cops had just rousted his son for possession of marijuana. On other occasions a knock had been the introduction for burglars and armed robbers. And, of course, the cops always knocked, unless they had a hot warrant—in which case they smashed your door down and knocked on your head. In any event, a knock on the door was to be treated with caution.

From behind his locked door, Dupaloff asked, "Who is it?"

"Police," Shapiro answered.

"Police? Again? What is it this time?"

"Just open the door, Dupaloff."

They heard the click of the deadbolt and the rattle of the chain being released. The door opened an inch, and they were observed by one bloodshot eye peering at them through the crack of the opening.

"We need to talk to you again," Shapiro said to the eye.

"You're not the same cops that were here before."

"We're from uptown. Open up."

70

"Let's see some identification," Dupaloff demanded bravely. "You don't look like no cops!"

"He wants to see our identification. Show it to him, Mc-Curdy."

McCurdy required no further stimulus. He stepped forward and launched his bulk against the door, causing it to fly open and in the process knocking Dupaloff onto his back, fracturing his nose and sending forth a gush of bright blood down his face and chest. Dupaloff struggled to sit upright, and groped for a handkerchief in his back pocket. The thought of identification fled his mind as McCurdy jerked him to his feet and then slammed him against the wall, his feet dangling a good foot above the floor. With his free hand McCurdy searched for a weapon, and, finding none, turned to Shapiro. "He's clean."

McCurdy lowered Dupaloff to the floor and stepped back. Dupaloff finally freed his handkerchief and began dabbing at the slowing flow of crimson. Shapiro watched him, giving him time to adjust to the situation.

"Now we can talk," he told Dupaloff. "Cooperate and he won't hurt you anymore."

Dupaloff looked at Shapiro with dread in his eyes. He knew these two weren't cops. "What do you want?" he managed to squeak. He turned to McCurdy. "You broke my nose."

"Big deal," McCurdy replied. "Sit down!"

Dupaloff sat on a kitchen chair that McCurdy pushed in his direction. "Let me get a wet towel," he said plaintively. "I'm still bleeding."

"Use your fucking shirt," Shapiro ordered. "We don't have time to play nurse to you."

"Bastards," Dupaloff muttered as he pulled his shirt from his pants and began wiping his face. Outside he could hear the sounds of traffic and people, but in his apartment he could only hear the crashing beat of his heart. He heard a police siren and thought of the old line about cops never being around when you need one.

Shapiro interrupted his reverie. "Where's Leo Baratto?"

"How the hell do I know?" He didn't understand why everyone thought he was supposed to know where one tenant was at any point in the day or night.

"He lives here, don't he?" McCurdy asked.

"He rents an apartment here. There's a difference. Besides, I don't keep track of where the tenants go."

"He's your drinking buddy, ain't he?" Shapiro asked. "Don't act like you don't know him pretty good."

"Yeah, we have a few drinks now and then, but I don't really know him all that good." Dupaloff was feeling more courage now that the line of questioning was about someone other than himself, and it was obvious that they didn't know much more than he did.

"You and him been pretty tight ever since he moved in."

"That doesn't mean I know him real good," Dupaloff protested truthfully.

He did not want to tell them that Baratto had been his main source of booze and that in return he provided Leo with a safe storage place for things Baratto didn't want to keep in his apartment. Like that package of heroin in the closet, not six feet from where Shapiro stood glaring down at him.

Dupaloff had quickly figured out what was in the package, and although he didn't use drugs, he knew that it was worth big money on the streets. And if Baratto had gotten himself into trouble with the cops and with these two guys, well, then, it was only right that he made a few bucks from the heroin. Besides, it was Baratto's fault that he was sitting here with a busted beak, wasn't it?

Recalling the police seal on the door of Baratto's apartment, Shapiro asked Dupaloff what he had told the police.

"I didn't tell them nothing! They just wanted to search Leo's place."

"You must have told them something," McCurdy said, and then, in a casual manner and without warning, brought his right hand across the left side of Dupaloff's head, tipping the chair over and depositing Dupaloff again on the floor, this time holding his head instead of his nose.

Shapiro waited while McCurdy picked Dupaloff up and set the chair upright and dumped Dupaloff into it. "What did you tell the cops?"

"I told them that he lived here," Dupaloff responded, holding his left hand to the side of his head. "That's all I said," he added, now eyeing the knife that had appeared in McCurdy's beefy hand. "Don't fuck around with that knife," he said to McCurdy, who ignored him.

"What else?"

"About his girl, too. The one he's been shacking up with. Cheryl something or other. You guys should ask her where he's at."

"We already have," McCurdy said.

"Exactly what did the cops ask you about Baratto?"

Dupaloff hesitated. He pulled the bloodstained shirt away from his face. The jolt delivered to his head by McCurdy had restarted the flow of blood. He wiped at his face again, thinking maybe he'd better go along with these two apes. The one with the blade looks like he'd slice me up good, Dupaloff thought. And enjoy it, too. Maybe if he gave them Leo's package they would go and leave him alone. Anyway, there wasn't enough of the stuff there to get hurt over.

"You mean that stuff about the dope? Is that what this is about?"

"Tell us about the dope," Shapiro said, his voice soft and reassuring. "Where did Leo keep it at?"

"The cops found some when they shook his place down. They asked me if he was pushing that shit."

"How much did they find?"

"Not much, just a little package."

"Where did he keep the rest of it?"

Dupaloff looked at them, trying to read their expressions. Looking at their eyes, he couldn't make heads or tails of what he saw. Baratto had told him one night that he had a lot of dope, but Dupaloff had never seen very much of it. Maybe he did have a bigger stash someplace. It shouldn't hurt Leo if he gave these guys the little package, and maybe Leo would be grateful and cut him in on some of the bigger stash. He decided to do it. These guys might even reward him for the package, and he could collect from both ends!

"Well, I'd be in big trouble with Leo, you know, if I said anything. But maybe we can make a deal, huh?"

"What kind of a deal?" Shapiro asked.

"If I knew where he kept the stuff, you could cut me in and give me a nice piece of money, right?"

McCurdy looked at Shapiro and smiled. He turned to Dupaloff. "Yeah, we'll take good care of you, you'll get a big cut."

"I can't afford any trouble with Baratto," Dupaloff said. "He's a real mean bastard when he's crossed."

"Listen," Shapiro told him. "He's got more trouble than he can handle right now. Just like you're going to have if you keep fucking around!" Shapiro took his hand out of his pocket and let Dupaloff see the knife. McCurdy knew what to expect. He put his own knife away.

"All right, all right, don't—just take it easy with that goddamned knife! I keep Leo's stuff for him, right here. He had me hold it in case someone came around his place looking for it."

"Where is it?" Shapiro asked, his voice very tight.

"We got a deal, right?" Dupaloff asked. "I mean, I should get something for the risk in holding it and having to answer to Leo. The cops would have found it when they shook his place down. We got a deal, right?"

The knife in Shapiro's hand moved so very quickly that for a moment Dupaloff didn't realize he'd been cut. The surgical steel had left a thin line across Dupaloff's left cheek, from his temple to the jawline. At first it was bloodless, then it ran red and the pain seemed to flow in unison with the blood, a fierce pain, like fire. Dupaloff jerked his hand up to his face in openmouthed amazement and was both surprised and shocked to see the blade flash again, opening up the back of the hand he had put to his face. He brought it down and stared at it, at the bones gleaming white and turning red. He was very, very scared. He realized that this could be it, he could die right here in this fucking chair! And he knew that Shapiro would not hesitate to slice him into bits and that he would probably enjoy doing so. He surrendered. Nothing was worth feeling that knife again.

"Now where is it?" Shapiro demanded. "Don't make me angry with you."

Dupaloff's fear grew then. This bastard had cut him twice without being angry! What would the prick do if he got mad? Fuck Leo and his dope and the money too. "It's in a shoe box on the closet shelf," he said, nodding toward the closet door. "Just don't cut me anymore. Please."

McCurdy opened the closet and took down the box and brought it to the couch, where he turned it upside down and watched the small bag of heroin bounce around. He picked it up and handed it to his boss. "Less than a fucking ounce here!" he exclaimed.

Dupaloff watched as Shapiro hefted the bag in his hand and then dropped it into his jacket pocket. Shapiro and McCurdy exchanged glances. Dupaloff thought it was finally over, they had what they wanted and would leave. Accordingly, he was surprised to hear Shapiro ask him where the rest of the dope was hidden. And riding fast after his surprise came the fear.

"That's all there is! Honest!" he nearly shouted, staring at the knife.

"Hold him," Shapiro ordered McCurdy, who forced

Dupaloff back into the chair, holding his arms while Shapiro stepped forward. Dupaloff was no longer afraid. He was terrified. He felt the hot, wet flood of his own urine racing down his legs. He heard himself babbling and pleading that he knew nothing more, and all the while he saw the shiny blade flash out at him, opening wound after wound. As he sank from the chair into blackness, his last sight was the smile on Shapiro's face.

4

amela Eling, who had dated Walter Sullivan regularly while he was a patient at the hospital, lived across from what had once been Tinker Park in Crystal, where area mothers had taken their children to play before the city ran a freeway through most of it and erected a shopping mall over the remainder. They had, however, spared a small section that now comprised a few scraggly trees, sparse, brownish grass, and several old benches left from better days. In those days the benches had been bright green. Now they were grayish with age and pigeon shit.

The mothers now took their offspring to Evans Park, several blocks east, and brought the family dog to Tinker Park, where the canines evacuated their bowels from one end of the park to the other, causing night users of the park never to be able to walk in a straight line.

Pamela Eling was in her late thirties, wearing a sundress with a flowered pattern that accented her thinness. She was about five feet seven inches tall, with the flat figure of a boy. She wore her dark hair tied back, which accentuated her sharp cheekbones and large hawklike nose. She stared at them with blue eyes red from crying.

"What is it?" she asked.

Her voice was warm and husky, filled with a promise that didn't match her appearance. "Miss Eling," Lonto began, showing her his badge, "I'm Detective Lonto and this is my partner, Detective Runnion. We'd like to talk with you for a few minutes, if we can."

"I suppose it's about Wally," she said. "Come in, please."

"How did you learn about Walter Sullivan?" Lonto asked her.

"A friend called me from the hospital this morning. I just can't believe it. He was such a nice man."

"How long had you known him?"

"I knew him for three years and dated him for two years. Can you tell me what happened?"

"He was murdered," Lonto answered. "When did you see him last?"

"Just last Sunday. I had a free afternoon and we drove out to the lake for a picnic."

"Did you talk to him after that?"

"He called me early Monday evening, about seven, I should think."

"How did he sound to you?"

"He seemed really cheerful, like . . ."

"Yes?"

"Like he was excited about something, a business deal he always spoke of."

"Do you know if this deal was with Leo Baratto?"

"Yes, it was. But Wally never would tell me what the deal was about."

"What did he tell you about it?"

"Wally dreamed a lot," she said. "His dream was that he and Leo were going to make one business deal and he— Wally, that is—would then buy a horse ranch and live happily ever after, as the story goes. He could talk for hours about ranches and mustang horses. But that's all it was, just dreams of fresh air and open spaces and the mountains. It was compensation, I think, for the harsh reality of blindness and city life." She took out a handkerchief and dabbed at her eyes.

"Did you ever hear him and Baratto speak of drugs?"

She looked at them in surprise. "Wally didn't know anything about drugs," she replied, nearly indignantly. "They never spoke of it or used drugs, not in my presence. But you must understand, it was always Wally and me, never the three of us. You see, I didn't like Leo."

"Did Wally have any friends other than Leo?" Lonto wanted to know.

"Wally didn't make friends easily. He was unsure of people because he was blind. It embarrassed him, and he resented pity."

"Do you know if he ever dated any of the other nurses at the hospital, or any other woman at all?" Runnion asked her. "Or had any visitors other than Leo?"

"Oh, I doubt it very much. It was a year before he would even ask *me* out. I don't think he dated anybody. He has a sister in Montana and she comes to see him—or came to see him—every year."

"How serious was the relationship between you and Wally, if I may ask?" Lonto inquired.

She sighed and looked at them with a small smile. "Look at me, Mr. Lonto. I'm thirty-seven, with a face and figure that have never made a man look at me twice. Most times, they never look once. With Wally, that had no importance. He couldn't use those artificial measurements and had only the things we shared to make a decision and base his feelings on. I loved him very much and I think he loved me."

"Had he any enemies you're aware of?"

"He never mentioned any. Why would he have enemies? He was a beautiful and gentle man, and few blind people go about making enemies."

"Just how well did he get along with Leo Baratto?"

"Oh, they never seemed to be really friends, not the way you would imagine friends to be, you know? They had more arguments than I can remember, yet they always stuck together. It was almost as if they had to remain together, no matter what happened between them. A bond that their arguments couldn't break."

"Perhaps that business deal?" Lonto suggested.

"Perhaps, yes, that is quite possible."

"Thank you for your time and help," Lonto said to her. "You have anything, Pat?"

"No, I guess that's it. Miss Eling, thank you again."

"Please let me know if his sister claims his body," Pamela Eling told them.

Back outside, as they walked to the car, Runnion asked, "What do you think?"

"I don't know," Lonto replied. "On the one hand, we have a dead blind vet who seems to have been a pretty decent guy, and on the other we have Leo Baratto, who's typical street crap. And we've got a probable heroin connection between them. About the only thing that can help us make any gain is a long talk with Baratto."

"Fat chance of him giving us anything!" Runnion said.

"Maybe we'll pick up something on the street," Lonto said. "I can't believe that there's top-flight smack out there and nobody is talking it up! It doesn't make sense to me. Doesn't it bother you?"

"Yeah," Runnion replied. "Somebody is always talking about the next shipment, next week, tomorrow, and so on. But not now."

It was almost six in the evening when they reached the station and checked out for the day. Runnion walked to the crosstown bus line and Lonto went to the parking ramp for his car. He wondered how Robin had spent her day.

He had not spoken with Robin since Wednesday night. Usually during the course of a day he would find or make time to call her or drop in to see her whenever his work took him near her apartment. And, of course, he spent his free evenings with her; their respective schedules seldom gave them many nights together.

He had met her through a friend at a party and had asked her out. Since then, they had shared what time they had free together. He honestly wished that she would quit her airline job and work within the city. He loved her and wanted to spend as much time with her as possible. He just had that one hangup which kept them apart, his fear of possible pain for her. Too many cops leave widows behind, and fatherless kids.

Thinking about her, he wondered why life and falling in love had to be so goddamned complicated. After all, he could just as easily have gone into another line of work, a normal job with normal hours and a normal life expectancy. All of which would allow him to have the type of life, yes, the normal life, of husband and father.

But Robin had always said, in their arguments on the subject, that nobody was guaranteed anything in life and you had to go with what you had. Her plane could fly into a mountain at any moment, but that would never prevent her from marrying before the crash. Lots of policemen were married, and the percentage of widows was actually quite small. He glanced at his watch, recalling his promise to her that he would think seriously about marriage.

When he reached her apartment building in Highland Park, the evening rush hour was over and the streets were quiet. He parked and locked the car. The building was old but well kept, with large elm trees in the yard and flower beds bordering the walkways and along the building's foundation. A few tenants had their windows open and he could hear kids laughing. He went up the steps quickly to the second floor and halted outside her door.

He knocked softly. A moment later he heard footsteps, then the door opened, the special, heavy-duty door chain preventing further movement. He had bought and installed the chain. She glanced out at him, closed the door, and then opened it wide, holding her arms out, a smile on her lips for him.

She was wearing a man's long-sleeved shirt, a blue-and-white plaid flannel that had faded to powder blue. She had borrowed it from his closet one night to use as a nightgown. She had laid claim to it ever since. Her hair was loose and in soft waves. He closed the door and she came into his arms and pressed her lips to his.

After a long minute, he pulled back and said his first words to her. "I think you might have missed me." She wiggled her nose at him and led him to the couch in the living room.

"I was wondering when you'd get off tonight. You didn't call all day!"

"It was more of a madhouse than usual," he told her. "Are you sure that's my shirt you've got on? I don't remember all those curves and bumps!"

"You've got a one-track mind, Lonto," she said, joining him on the couch. "Those curves and bumps are all me, no shirt."

"I should check, just to make sure."

She shook her head.

"No checking, huh?"

"Nope."

"How come?"

"We need to talk," she said. "It's important that we talk, seriously."

"What about?"

She looked at him closely. There was sadness in her eyes now. She raised an eyebrow expectantly. Lonto, knowing what she wanted to discuss, spoke. "About us, huh? I have been thinking about us, Robin. I think about us and marriage and having kids all the time. I just don't know what to do about it."

She took his hand and held it tightly in hers. "Pat is married, isn't he?"

"You know he is."

"How many of the detectives you know are married?"

He thought about it for a moment. "I guess all of them, except me."

She smiled at him. "I just happen to know that over sixty percent of all police officers are married."

"Yeah?" Lonto countered. "Well, I just happen to know that cops have the highest divorce rate, too."

She rose and then sat on his lap. Unexpectedly, she began to cry and he said, "Come on, Robin. Don't cry. You know it drives me nuts."

She nodded, and continued to cry.

"You've really been carrying this around in your mind a lot, haven't you? You've got your heart set on it."

"Yes," she sniffed.

"You know what a cop's life is like, and the pay isn't that great."

She nodded again, her face buried in his neck.

"You'll worry about me all the time," he added.

"I worry about you now," she said into his ear.

"I suppose you know I really do love you," he said. "So if it's all that important to you, I think we should get married."

She stopped crying and lifted her face to his. "Is that a proposal?"

"Of course it is! Will you marry me?"

"Are you really sure you want to?"

He looked into her eyes for a long moment. "Yes, I'm sure. How about it?"

"Yes! Yes! When?"

"You pick the date," he said, matching her ear-to-ear grin with one of his own. "I still have all of my vacation time left. We can do it whenever you wish."

She seemed on the verge of further tears. He pulled her close and whispered, "I mean it, Robin. I've thought about it and I don't want to lose you. If you're willing to marry a cop, then I'm your guy."

She smiled and nodded, the tears welling in her eyes. She wiggled on his lap.

"That," he informed her, "will get you into trouble!"

"I certainly hope so," She grinned. "I'd hate to waste a perfectly good wiggle!"

"You've never wasted one that I'm aware of. Are you one of those nympho types I've heard about?"

"There's only one way to find out," she told him. They reached simultaneously for each other's hands and, without words, walked toward her bedroom.

Nicki had learned early in her career as a hooker that for a working girl to survive on the streets, she had to take advantage of the opportunities that came her way. Her first pimp, for instance, had schooled her in how to relieve drunken johns of wallets, rings, watches, and other valuables, and to pass those windfalls on to him. After several months of that one-sided relationship with him, she had realized that she could take better care of herself and her habit if she didn't simultaneously take care of him and his. She promptly dumped him. Shortly thereafter, he was arrested for beating another girl and was sent to prison and out of her life altogether.

Nicki had also come to realize that she could rarely afford the luxury of friends, lovers, or anything else in her life other than her habit. Heroin had become her friend and lover, and it was her passport into a life more beautiful than she had known before her addiction.

It was simple escape, from failed friends and faithless lovers, from hard luck and bad times and the subtle self-contempt that all hookers harbor deep within. With the heroin coursing through her system, even being a hooker wasn't any longer quite as numbing. And when she was high, even a drunken trick could be imagined as a rich and skilled lover who would make her happy ever after—or least until the false euphoria in her blood died out and it was time for another fix.

It was not surprising, then, that when she learned there was a tidy stack of five-hundred-dollar bills waiting to be claimed by the person knowing the whereabouts of one Leo Baratto, she quickly sought out Shapiro. She had managed to pinch a nice piece of Baratto's heroin and hide it, and she knew that just as she didn't really care for or about him, neither did he care for or about her. She had to look out for herself. With the money she had already, the heroin, and now a chance at a big-money deal, she would be very well off for a long time.

She found Shapiro, accompanied as usual by McCurdy, in Dirty Joe's, a bar frequented by hookers. She joined them at their table. Shapiro and his Godzilla had recently finished the evening rounds, making the collection and—a rarity—not having felt it necessary to strike even one person. They were relaxing and having a quiet drink while discussing what to do next in the search for Leo Baratto.

During a passionate point he was making to McCurdy, Shapiro realized someone was standing next to the table. He fell silent and looked up to see a pretty young blonde looking down at him. A split-second before he could speak, she opened the conversation.

"I understand you're looking for someone, Mr. Shapiro. I might be able to help you. May I sit down?"

Shapiro, to McCurdy's mild surprise, rose, pulled a chair out from the table, helped the woman into it, and signaled the bartender. The bartender scurried over and Shapiro stopped him in his tracks with one brief order. "Champagne, now!"

"Well, young lady, who is that you think I'm looking for?" Shapiro said after the champagne was poured and the bartender had moved off.

"Well, I don't know for certain that it is you who are looking for him," Nicki replied. "I just heard that it might be very worthwhile to somebody who knew where Leo Baratto was staying."

Shapiro and McCurdy exchanged brief glances. "Haven't I seen you around?" Shapiro asked.

"Probably," Nicki said. "I usually work out of Anna's Massage, Mr. Shapiro—on the out-call service. I'm Nicki."

"Smart girl," Shapiro observed to McCurdy. "Maybe we could use a sharp, good-looking lady to manage one of the parlors, huh, McCurdy?"

"I think you might have something there, boss."

"Yeah. Maybe one of the places in the suburbs. Does that sound like something that might interest you, Nicki?"

"Yes, yes it does, Mr. Shapiro."

Shapiro reached over and grabbed her arm in a sudden and painful grip. "On the other hand," he hissed at her, "if you're not smart and are feeding me a line, you might end up with a face your mama wouldn't look at, let alone love, and you'll be selling your ass in a dark alley for two bucks a pop!"

"Please," Nicki begged, trying to free her arm from Shapiro's tight grip. "I'm not lying, I know where Leo is right now!"

"Where?" Shapiro demanded.

"He's at my apartment. Just a few blocks from here. I told him I had to go out on a call and he said he'd wait for me to return. I can take you there."

Shapiro smiled and released her arm, rubbing it lightly and giving it a pat before allowing her to pull it to her side, where she too rubbed it. "I guess you are a smart girl after all, Nicki. You just write down the address for me now." He gave her a pen and a matchbook and watched her write.

"Pay the lady, McCurdy," Shapiro said when Nicki gave him the pen and matchbook. "You just sit right here and enjoy yourself until we return, Nicki."

Nicki watched McCurdy count bills and lay a small pile in front of her. "About that job, Mr. Shapiro. I'd really like that, and I'd do a real good job for you."

"I know you will," Shapiro told her as he rose to leave. "After we talk with Leo, I'll give you a call here. I've got something really special in mind for you."

"Thanks, Mr. Shapiro," Nicki said, and watched as they headed for the door. She was elated, almost high. She knew that now she was going to have it made in this city. With a guy like Shapiro behind her, she couldn't miss.

Never let it be said that an unusual homicide, that of a blind man, for instance, can't lead to bigger and better things. Or at least to some fairly bizarre events and facts to confuse the police. In this, the land of the free and several million crazies, anything can and usually does happen. Some homicide cases can give even the best cop a bleeding ulcer, because the more you seem to learn about a case, the less you seem to know. As a case in point, Lonto and Runnion sat in a corner of the squad room on Friday morning and tried to figure out just what it was that they knew, or seemed to know.

To begin with, they had a great deal of information on Sullivan and Baratto from various military, civilian, and police records, as well as from those with whom they had discussed both men—Pamela Eling, for instance. Unfortunately, they were of the opinion that what they did have didn't seem to add up to much. Take Walter Sullivan. All of their collected data on him indicated that he had never been arrested for anything in his life. His military record was spotless and positive, and he had served his country in such a manner as to have received several letters of commendation and four decorations for outstanding service in combat. He had been, from all available indications, a recruiting officer's example of a model career soldier.

With that information, Lonto and Runnion had found it difficult to connect him logically with such an opposite and disparate type as Leo Baratto in some deal that involved very high-grade heroin, a deal that had culminated, for Sullivan, in a vicious death.

They also had a great deal of information about Leo Baratto, and every bit of it pointed to him as an outstanding example of a career street punk. His police rap sheet included arrests for assault, theft, burglary, and simple robbery, with convictions only for theft and one assault. The rap sheet and investigative reports rated him as a prime rat, and all signs pointed to his eventually receiving, at best, a long prison term. He was not one of the police department's favorite people.

Judging by the records, he was not one of the United States Army's pets, either. His service record revealed a series of court-martials, stockade time, and simple unit penalties. At the time he had been wounded, with Sullivan, and returned to the States, he had been very close to receiving a dishonorable discharge as an undesirable. Leo had been exactly the type of soldier and person whom Sullivan would logically have steered well clear of.

But logic, it appeared, had not applied to the relationship between Sullivan and Baratto. It didn't make a hell of a lot of sense to Lonto or Runnion, no matter how they cut it up and dished it out. They were very interested in putting Baratto on the hot spot and forcing him to make sense out of it all.

Lonto, sitting behind his desk, closed the thick and growing case file and wished he were in bed with Robin instead of reading histories and reports that didn't add up right. A man should be with his woman, and future wife, on the day before she flew off to faraway places again. He tapped the file, lightly at first, and then in a steady staccato.

"What do you think, Pat?" he finally asked, much to Runnion's relief, since the drumming of Lonto's fingers on the file had begun to grate on his nerves.

"The only sensible thing that ties them together is the heroin."

"And being army buddies, wounded together."

"A career sergeant and a jailbird as buddies?" Runnion asked. "Really?"

"Well, they sure as hell have been close since Nam."

"I still think it's just the heroin," Runnion said. "If Sullivan had it and Baratto knew it, he would suck up to Sullivan until he had a shot at the stash."

Lonto shrugged. "So far we've turned up seven or eight grams of high-grade junk. And maybe there was room for two or three ounces in the bottom of that duffel bag. Even at current street prices, that's damn slim money for Baratto to wait for over a period of years, and then butcher a man to get it."

"Maybe there's more. A lot more."

"You sure know how to cheer me up, Pat. There's really not a hell of a lot more we can do right now except keep looking for Baratto. We have an all-points on him. We need to find out what the street rap is on him and Shapiro. While we're at that, we can ask around about any word on a new smack supply."

"I wonder if we should bring Narcotics in on this, Tony."

"Let's say we did. What the hell do we have to give them? Only guesses."

"That stuff tested out pure, Tony."

"I know. And it looks like it came straight from Asia. But we just don't have enough to turn over to them. Besides, it isn't simply a dope case, we've got a murder on our hands, and that either makes this case ours or keeps us on it. The heroin is secondary. It might be the sole motive, sure, but this isn't just a dope case. If we bring in the narcs, we invite all those assholes to stir the waters and maybe prevent us from solving the murders. You anxious to try to get rid of this case, Pat?"

"Well, we are up to our asses in cases and we're putting in a lot of time on this one. But the reason I think Narcotics should be brought in is that we can use some help, and they do know the dope scene better than we do."

"We can always use help," Lonto agreed. "And maybe down the line we'll have to call them in, but for now I think we should continue as is."

"Is one of you men Detective Lonto?" asked a voice in the doorway of the squad room. A small woman in a short blue dress stood there. She was perhaps twenty-five years old and had the kind of clean and natural beauty that could make all bachelors ponder the prospects of wedded bliss. She was simply beautiful, and she seemed sensitive enough to be aware of the impact she had upon men. Her hair was a very rich copper color, and it framed her delicate-featured face and large blue eyes. Her mouth was perfectly molded and she wore no lipstick—didn't need any, in fact—and she had a fair complexion with a slight tan. She stood there with the blue sundress clinging lightly and suggestively to her breasts and hips, and gave the detectives an excellent view of her long legs. She looked from one to the other and smiled hopefully.

"I'm Lonto," Tony said, trying to clear his throat.

She walked into the room and seated herself directly in front of his desk. She smiled at Runnion and then turned it on Lonto and extended her right hand to him. "I'm Faith Sullivan. The officer at the desk said that you men are investigating my brother's murder."

"Yes, that's right, Miss Sullivan," said Lonto, accepting her hand and noticing the warmth in it. "This is my partner, Pat Runnion. I didn't know your brother had any relatives in town."

"I flew in from Montana last night," she informed them. "They notified me about Wally on Tuesday evening, and I came as soon as I could."

"Please allow me to extend my sympathy, Miss Sullivan. I know this must be a very painful time for you." Lonto said.

"That goes for me, too, miss," Runnion added.

"Thank you, gentlemen, I appreciate it."

"Miss Sullivan, I should tell you that we have positively identified your brother's remains and there is no need for you to go through that ordeal," Lonto said.

"Please, call me Faith. I came, of course, to arrange for Wally to return home with me and to claim his effects. I also want to know if you have arrested his killer."

Lonto looked out the window. "Not yet," he told her. "We have your brother's property here, and his body, too, of course."

"Is his Bible among his property? He wanted me especially to have it, and it's not at his apartment."

Lonto and Runnion exchanged a glance, then Lonto replied. "I don't recall seeing a Bible in his effects. Is it of value? I mean, like a rare book?"

"Oh, I don't really know. I doubt it. It's just that Wally wrote me, or had his nurse write for him, and he said that if anything happened to him during his last operation, his Bible would be given to me. I was to keep it until his business partner contacted me. Apparently it was of value to his partner."

"Did he mention why the Bible was of interest to his partner?" Lonto asked her. "What exactly were you supposed to do with the Bible?"

She looked at them thoughtfully. "He just wrote that it was important to his partner, and that if he died in the hospital the Bible would be sent to me. I think if I had the Bible, the partner would be sure that I received Wally's share of the business they invested in. But then, Wally didn't die in the hospital."

"Did he ever indicate to you what he and his partner had invested in?" Runnion asked. "Or anything about his partner?"

"Just his name and address. A Leo Baratto, and he lives in an awful place across town from here," she said. "He's not there now."

"Miss Sullivan—" Lonto began.

"Please. Call me Faith. 'Miss Sullivan' sounds like an elderly schoolteacher."

Lonto cleared his throat again. "Faith, we have good reason to believe Leo Baratto was involved in your brother's murder. We have a warrant for his arrest. If you have any idea at all where he might be, please tell us."

"I have only the address. I don't know him or where he might be. He lives on Cedar Avenue."

"Yes, we know."

"Was Wally involved in something illegal, Mr. Lonto?"

Lonto shifted in his chair. It's tough, he thought, to tell someone that a loved one has been murdered. It's tougher telling them the deceased was also involved in something shady that led to the death. It is even tougher to have to tell a beautiful young woman, one with the kind of loveliness that often makes men think the woman is fragile and will likely shatter in the face of harsh and ugly reality.

92

"We think," Lonto said softly, "that it's possible he was. The man he called his business partner is a known criminal with a long record."

"What was Wally involved in?"

"There is evidence to indicate that narcotics are involved, and that another murder might very well be connected."

"Oh," she said, very softly, and lowered her eyes.

"What made you ask the question, Faith?" Lonto asked. "Did he mention drugs or anything like that when you visited him at the hospital?"

"I just knew," she replied. "It was like that ever since he was wounded and lost his sight. He was very bitter about the war and didn't think we should have been involved there— even before he was hurt. Afterwards, he was *very* bitter and often told me that it didn't matter, that the army was going to make him very rich in payment for his eyesight."

"Did he mean his pension or the disability pay he got?"

She shook her head. "No. He meant a *lot* of money. Enough to buy a horse ranch for us. That's what he wanted. A ranch."

"How much does a ranch cost?" Runnion asked.

"A lot," she answered. "So much that I thought sometimes it could only be a dream to him."

"Could you be more precise as to the cost?" Lonto asked.

"Is it important?"

"It might be," Lonto said. "It could provide us with an idea of what he had to sell or trade for that amount of cash."

"Like drugs?"

Lonto nodded.

"The place Wally always talked about would cost over three hundred thousand dollars." She paused and looked at them thoughtfully. "He would joke about it, saying that after he got out of the hospital he would buy two or three places just like it. Is there really that much money paid for drugs? Wally really wasn't dreaming?"

"A vast amount of money is spent daily on narcotics," Lonto told her. "I wish we knew for sure whether he was dreaming or not."

"You don't think he was, do you?"

"No, I don't." Lonto sighed. "The drugs that were found in your brother's apartment were very unusual. If there were enough, your brother could have bought his ranch, and Buckingham Palace too. They are quite probably the reason why he was killed. I really hope that the ranch was simply the desperate dream of a sightless man. But I don't believe it was."

"I don't think so either," Faith said. "When we talked, it seemed like it was. But ever since he came back, that was the one thing he always spoke of, as though if it were a dream, he knew that it would come true. He was very confident of that."

"Did he ever mention anything about how he was going to buy the ranch?"

"Only that he and Leo Baratto would have lots of money once he left the hospital. It seemed that whatever they were doing, they needed each other to do it. He joked about it once, saying that no matter how long it was before he left the hospital, his partner would wait."

"Did he say why?"

"I had the impression that Leo had to wait, because without Wally, there wouldn't be any business."

"Sounds like each had something the other needed," Runnion observed.

"And maybe Baratto has everything now," Lonto said. He paused a long moment. "Miss Sullivan—uh, Faith—your brother had been hospitalized for several years. Was there any medical reason for his being in that particular hospital? Like special treatment provided solely by this hospital?"

She shook her head. "No. Nothing like that. *I* wanted Wally to transfer to the VA hospital nearer to home, so I could be with him more often. It's in Helena. Wally always said he had to stay here."

"Did he indicate why?"

"Just that they had to be here, he and Leo. I have a problem in accepting that Wally was involved in drugs."

"We don't know that for sure," Lonto reminded her. "All we know is that some drugs were found in the apartment he rented. They could have belonged to someone else."

"I'd like to see him, Mr. Lonto."

"He's at the morgue, Faith. In homicide cases an autopsy is mandatory."

"I want to see him. I must be certain it's him."

"We're positive it is your brother, Faith. He died a violent death, and I don't think you should see the results."

"I have to see him," she answered. She was straightfaced, sober and sad.

"Pat, would you get the car?"

The morgue was the last place you'd want to take somebody, especially a pretty young girl whose brother now looked as if he had had his chest run over by a wild lawn mower. It was a chilly and cheerless place at any time. The very feeling of death permeated one's core, and the imagery of cold, dead bodies pigeonholed in the walls kept even veteran officers from entering the place unless a visit was unavoidable.

A built-in destruct device in each of us, like those tape recorders on the old "Mission Impossible" series, would be a blessing to humanity, eliminating places like morgues and their creep-show atmosphere. And one could avoid having to deal with morgue attendants, people made callous by the constant exposure to death, who have numbed their sensitivities and who come across as indifferent, even cynically blasé.

"Sullivan," Lonto said to the attendant. "Water Sullivan."

"We already sent you guys our report."

"Yes, I have it. We're here to see Mr. Sullivan."

"Okay," the attendant said, picking up a clipboard and running a finger down a list. "Sullivan, Walter B. That him?"

"How many Sullivans do you have down here?"

"Just him."

"Then don't you think it's logical he's the one?" Lonto asked, disliking the man on sight.

"Yeah. Well, he's over here. We keep all the stiffs we're finished with in this section," the attendant said, leading them toward the other side of the room and through a door into one of the vaults where the dead awaited the arrival of a hearse from some funeral home.

The vault was surprisingly dry, no sense of the expected clamminess and chill. But it was stark, the air nearly reeking of sterility and antiseptics. It was not a room for the living.

The attendant stopped before a drawer with a tag reading SULLIVAN WALTER B. He opened the door and slid the body tray out. The tray was followed by a soft rush of cold air that immediately sank into one's bones, causing an involuntary shiver. The attendant pulled away the sheet covering Walter Sullivan, and they were suddenly staring at the ugly rawness of his lacerated chest. Beside him, Lonto heard Faith stifle a choked cry and felt her turn her back on her brother's remains.

"Faith," Lonto said softly, "is that Walter?"

"Yes," she choked. "My God, what happened to him?"

"We think he was tortured."

"Oh, my God," Faith muttered.

Lonto nodded to the attendant, who covered the body again and quietly slid the tray back into the dark tomb and closed the door.

"Are you all right?" Lonto asked her.

"What?"

"Are you okay?"

"I think so," she whispered. "Please, take me out of here."

Lonto took her arm and steered her to the exit. There was a sour taste in his mouth, and he could feel her body trembling as she walked beside him, Runnion trailing by a step or two.

5

There is a certain point in the course of a case when the investigating detectives decide that the case has developed enough that they should present it to their superiors. Often that point is arrived at simply because, like now, Lonto thought, the detectives are going in circles. The Sullivan case was ripe for dropping into the lap of Lieutenant Jaworski.

Jaworski was reading the case file with impatient interest, dividing his attention between reading and listening to the two detectives as they provided him with their views and the facts upon which they were based. Finally he closed the file and stared at them.

"Sometimes I wonder what the hell kind of shop I'm running!" he exclaimed. "I put the two most experienced detectives I've got on a homicide case with only one suspect.

We have all the information on this guy we need, and you can't pull this punk in? Instead you come up with another body and the theory that there's a large stash of pure heroin in town. Bring Baratto in and we'll worry about the heroin later. Is that asking too much?"

He sat behind his desk as he spoke to them. He was a broad-shouldered, heavy man, with a reddish face lined by years of resentment, suspicion, and high-blood pressure. He was losing his hair in a steady march toward baldness. His sharp blue eyes peered out from beneath rather shaggy eyebrows. He stared hardest at Lonto. He didn't like dago cops, which was not surprising in a Polish-American burdened with ethnic prejudices peculiar to most lower-class Americans, and exercised when they reach positions of authority. It is no different elsewhere, every country is the same, only the flags are different.

In the case of Lonto and Italians in general, Jaworski's bias stemmed from a long-ago incident when he was still a beat cop. He had been shot by a hood who happened to be of Italian extraction. While Jaworski realized that getting shot was something that went with the territory, the exact location of the wound was what evoked constant and painful memories. The bullet had severely damaged many of the nerves in his buttocks, causing him to stand far more often than the average American, and to spend, over the years, substantial sums on various devices claiming to provide the sitter with great relief. The cushion he sat on at the moment had cost him over a hundred dollars.

Lonto was his best cop, which meant Jaworski couldn't fuck him around or get rid of him, which made Jaworski resent Lonto all the more. Now, sitting on his expensive cushion, feeling, in fact, no pain, but ever aware of the threat of pain lying just beneath the next too-fast move on the cushion, Jaworski realized that the sight of Lonto standing before him, looking down on him seated on his reverse crown, as the station-house comedians had labeled his cushion, was more mental than physical pain. Lonto, being Italian, simply reminded him of his wound. But hell, Jaworski thought, Lonto isn't to blame. Too bad he isn't Polish, though.

"What about this hooker, this Emerson girl?" he finally asked. "Are you sure she doesn't know where Leo Baratto is?"

"Well," Lonto replied, "there's the chance, of course, that she does and is holding out, but I think it's more likely she expects him to contact her."

"What are you doing about it?"

"We'd like to get an extra man to stake out her place. Hell, we've got a patrolman sitting at Baratto's apartment now, let's pull him, put him in civvies and let him keep track of the Emerson girl. Baratto's more likely to show up around her than to return to his apartment."

"Yeah, there's not too much chance he'll go home, you think?"

"He's no intellectual, but he's got to know by now that we've been there and are watching the place. He's smart enough not to risk it."

Jaworski was now standing. "Let's do it, then," he said. "Just make sure that if he does show up at the girl's place, the patrolman knows he's to call in for backup. What are you two going to be doing?"

"I think our best bet is to work the streets for whatever information we can pick up or buy. There should be something out there on him or the heroin," Lonto replied.

Jaworski looked at Lonto, then at Runnion. A dago and a mick, he thought. What a pair. "Then why aren't you clowns out there getting the facts?" he asked, with the faked smile of the insincere man.

One thing common to police forces worldwide is the snitch system. It is, in point of fact, an operational necessity, for without informants over 80 percent of the cases police now marked as solved or closed would remain a mystery. In narcotics law enforcement, the percentage is far higher. Without the exchange of money, favors, or leniency for information, most police departments would be almost wholly ineffective in terms of solving crimes.

Detectives need informants the most, and they jealously guard their identities to keep them on their feet and on the street, obtaining information. Cops have been known to help their key snitches pay the rent, to get a case against them dropped or reduced in severity, and even to drop off some narcotics to junkies who have both the need for it and useful information. And they tacitly ignore the criminal actitivites their snitches are involved in, or use them as a lever against somebody who might be rather reluctant to divulge a secret or two. The arrangement is invariably a strict business relationship. Policemen, like most people, hold in contempt the snitch, the rat. They dislike them, on the whole, but value the working relationship.

One of Lonto's best informants happened to be one of those rare cases where the officer likes the informant, and there was mutual respect between the two men. In fact, this one gave Lonto information primarily out of his liking for him. Fostering that affection was the fact that Lonto had once been a Silver Street kid himself. The informant felt a touch of pride and admiration over the fact that Lonto had gone "the right way." Additionally, even when Tony Lonto was a tough street kid, he had protected the newsstand and person of Trash Can O'Toole. Lonto had liked O'Toole then, and still did.

The newsstand was located on the corner of Fourth Avenue and Silver Street, seven blocks north of the station house. On the way to see O'Toole, Lonto observed his old neighborhood with a jaundiced but tolerant eye. At a very rough guess, Lonto figured he probably could arrest three of

100

every four people he saw for some infraction of the law. In that neighborhood, being a pimp, a pusher, a junky, a prostitute, a mugger, or a general crook was almost a way of life. It was a veritable criminal culture, an economy based on crime, with a language and value system of its own.

Even those with a legitimate job or business, and no police record except a minor charge here and there, did something shady on the side. O'Toole ran his business just as he had for the past thirty years, and Lonto was aware that the old man was a moderately successful bookie in addition to tending the newsstand he called his "publishing operation." Lonto could not have cared less, even if O'Toole were to become the biggest bookie in town, just as long as he continued to fill Lonto's notebook with reliable information.

Lonto found O'Toole in his usual position, atop a high stool behind the counter of the stand. He was leafing through a copy of *Hustler* magazine, his mouth hanging open as he stared at a variety of T's and A's. "Don't you know looking at that stuff makes your hair fall out, Trash Can?" Lonto asked by way of greeting.

Trash Can rubbed his balding head. "Sure as hell does! Don't it?" He grinned. "How you doing, Tony?"

"Oh, I'm okay, I guess. But I really need some help. I need something on some local talent."

"Who?"

"Leo Baratto. Got anything?"

"Sure! Everyone around here is up on Big Time Leo. That's all I hear about lately, ever since he got out of the service, how he's going to be big time. Why you want to know?"

"We want him for murder one."

"Yeah," O'Toole said, shaking his head slowly. "I've heard about that, too. Real bad shit there, Tony. Real bad. But you got to realize that Leo's been talking that big-time shit for a long time now. No one believes the bastard anymore—if they ever did. Everybody talks that big-time bull-shit."

"So just what were Leo's big-time plans?"

"Far as I heard, he was supposed to have some very high-class smack for sale. Enough of it to set him up for life. But there's always talk like that around, too. You know that, Tony. And most of it comes from the vets back from Vietnam. The only souvenirs these guys seem to have from the war is either a habit or the shit for a habit. It must have been real cheap over there."

It made sense to Lonto. Street-wise kids exposed to the corruption of war, and the special corruptions that had permeated everything connected with Vietnam, turned to high-grade, powerful, and inexpensive drugs, and the desire to use them had destroyed tens of thousands of American boys. Fear and frustration lent their weight to tip the scales against the GIs. And those street guys had quickly seen the potential for large incomes in smuggling into the States some of the drugs they had tripped over in Asia. Some, a few of them, had observed that a military medical ship would be an ideal vehicle on which to ship home their contraband.

"A lot of guys brought drugs home," Lonto said. "It's been turning up in small amounts for a couple of years. Instead of throwing a beer bash, a lot of the Nam vets throw a smack party."

"Yeah," Trash Can agreed. "Only the word on Baratto is that he had a big chunk of shit for sale, and he had samples for anyone interested in making a big buy."

"He wasn't pushing?" Lonto asked with disbelief.

"No. He wasn't on the street with twenty-dollar bags. He was putting out the word that he had something sweet for a big buyer. From what I hear, he was either dealing or trying to deal with some heavyweights."

"Name them."

"Shit, Tony, you know better than me who runs the dope

down here. Shapiro and his playmate have had that sewed up for years. Anyway, all this is old news. Leo was only making those big-shot noises when he first came home."

"Nothing lately?"

Trash Can mulled that over for a minute. "Now that's strange, when you think about it," he said. "Baratto came back and made all that noise until he got the attention of Shapiro. After that, not a word about him having anything to sell. Now the word is that not only are you guys looking for him, but so is Shapiro."

"So maybe he sold what he had to Shapiro and didn't deliver?"

"Maybe. If he did, he's a great bullshit artist, because Shapiro and McCurdy sure have taken care of him, paying his bills, letting him run up a tab. I never knew those two to be friendly and generous with anybody they were finished doing business with."

"Yeah," Lonto mused. "Shapiro would get rid of a punk like Baratto in a hurry, unless Baratto still had something he wanted. Maybe they just got tired of paying his bills."

"Well, you know Baratto's quite a drinker. And he was talking about how tight he was with Shapiro. You know if that was false, Shapiro would've had McCurdy take his head off by now. Whadda you think?"

"I think Baratto still has something Shapiro wants. That's why they want him. Have you heard anything about heroin lately?"

"Just the usual junky talk."

"Like?"

"Like their connection was promising them all of the stuff they could buy, soon. They're living from shot to shot and the promise of a bonanza. That's standard shit, Tony. What you looking for, smack or Leo?"

"Baratto first," Lonto answered. "Any lead at all to where he's holed up. And whatever you pick up concerning a new supply of heroin on the street. Especially if it's supposed to be super-sweet."

"How bad you need this?"

"I need it yesterday, Trash Can. I need it as soon as you can get it to me. I've got a shitty feeling about this case. And if Shapiro and his ape are involved, I want to know. If *they* find Leo, we never will."

"Let me see what I can find out, Tony. If there's anything, I'll get back to you."

Detective Pat Runnion was spending his afternoon locating his first-class snitch, too. He was having some difficulty finding his man, because Bootleg Brady could never be counted upon to be located quickly. You could never hope to catch him in his one-room flop in one of the area's seediest "hotels," unless you lucked out because one of his pals had brought him home to sleep it off. Usually his drinking buddies simply propped him against a tree, in a doorway, or against some alley wall. In those cases, Bootleg always woke up soiled by his own vomit and urine, hung over and with his pockets turned inside out. Quite often his shoes were gone.

Bootleg Brady's life-style made it difficult to locate him, and his journeys also made him valuable to Runnion. Brady was one of those characters who is a permanent fixture in any big-city slum area or ghetto. People were used to his now-and-then presence and he was ignored to the point of nonexistence. Robberies were planned within earshot of him, pushers sold dope three feet from him, and hookers hooked their tricks close enough to him so that he smelled their perfumes and heard their deep-throated whispers of promised delight to hot-eyed johns just dying to unload their money and their passion in a fast and furtive rendezvous.

No one paid any attention to Brady, and he appreciated it. During each day and night's chore of drinking himself into oblivion, Brady heard and saw much of value to Runnion. As rum-sodden as Brady's brain must have been, his memory was exceptionally good, as though the sights and sounds that reached his senses somehow penetrated the haze of alcohol and impressed themselves into his data bank.

Runnion found the man a fascinating character, apart from the information he sold. Runnion knew, for instance, that the name on Brady's birth certificate was Daniel Eugene Brady, and that he received a monthly check from an address in Highland Park Heights, where the name Brady was synonymous with corporate power plays and great wealth.

Runnion had spent not a few hours speculating about that association. He wondered if this "town drunk" was the bastard son of a local tycoon. Or was the drunk himself the tycoon? Runnion never pressed Brady, however. He was sure that Brady enjoyed his life, actually liked drinking, and had no intention of doing anything else. The pain that had driven him to the bottle was apparently long dead, and he had simply adopted his way of life with open arms. If he had once had the pride necessary to be part of that particularly rich Brady family, there was no sign of it now. Brady could easily qualify if the *Guinness Book of World Records* ever established a category for greatest number of incidents of pocket-picking, hangovers, and times awakening to find oneself reeking of one's own urine and vomit.

Runnion decided that the best way to find Brady was to allow Brady to find *him*. So he stationed himself in the doorway of one the dives, and sure enough, not too long thereafter Brady came shuffling up the street and entered the bar, not indicating whether he had recognized Runnion. Runnion watched as Brady continued on to the men's room. Runnion went in and ordered a beer. When he was on his third one, Brady came out of the men's room and headed for a table.

Runnion watched him make his way to the tables along the wall. Brady was wearing his usual shirt-and-jeans combination, much like Runnion, who was hopeful that nobody would make him as a cop. No one in the bar, however, gave a shit who he was, as long as he kept out of their business.

There were six other men in the place, four at the bar and two sleeping in separate back booths. The men at the bar were engrossed in their drinks in a depressing silence. It was the sort of place where one came to get drunk, period. It was not a bar for socializing.

Runnion moved to Brady's table and sat down, beer in hand. Brady looked up at him. "You buying?" he asked. He was very thin, almost emaciated. His hair was wispy and gray, and a two-day growth of stubble gave him a decidedly grubby appearance. He was wearing dirty jeans and a black shirt. His eyes, as he looked at Runnion, waiting for an answer, were a washed-out light blue, buried in a face that featured high cheekbones and a pinched-in look. He looks, Runnion thought, like a nervous skeleton. He waved for the bartender.

"What are you drinking, Brady?"

"From you, I'll take a double bourbon. Several of them, in fact."

"A big double, bartender," Runnion said. He waited for the man to bring the drink and leave, and then watched Brady lift the glass gently to his eager lips. There was a real look of joy deep in Brady's eyes as the first hint of the whiskey reached his nervous system.

Brady put the glass down with a deep sigh. "Ahhh, that's real good!" he said, grinning at Runnion. "I wonder if my old drinking buddy, Leo, will be around today?" he asked to no one in particular. But Runnion knew he was being teased. In his comparative sobriety, Brady knew what Runnion was looking for.

"You have something about Baratto?"

"He's a drinker, ain't he?" Brady responded. "I know all the boozers on the strip. Especially those who like to talk and are willing to buy a guy a drink or two. Not like some people I know," Brady finished, staring pointedly at his empty glass.

"I think I get your message, Brady. You keep talking and I'll keep buying," Runnion told him, waving again at the bartender.

On his second bourbon, Brady said that if he were Baratto, he'd be very careful to stay off the streets and to hole up somewhere, real safe.

"Why?"

"Way I hear it, there's a lot of people looking for him 'cause they say there's some big money for whoever can tell Shapiro where to look."

"I have competition, huh?"

"Oh, yeah! And they pay better than you, Runnion! I understand Shapiro lent Baratto over two grand to live on, just a couple of weeks ago."

"Nobody in his right mind would give that punk two grand, or loan it to him. He must be holding something Shapiro wants bad."

"Well, certainly, Runnion! It's heroin, top-flight shit, so I hear."

"How much are we talking about?"

"Enough for several nice samples to pay back the loan, and a promise to deliver in pounds."

"Baratto tell you this?"

Brady grinned. "In bits and pieces. I helped him drink up his loan. He runs off at the mouth when he's boozed up good."

"And Shapiro gave him the two Gs?"

"Yup."

"And Shapiro is now offering nice money for Baratto's whereabouts?"

"Yup."

Runnion ran the conversation through his mind, but could

think of no questions that would augment his store of information, and slipped Brady a ten-spot.

"That all you got for me?" Brady demanded.

"Anybody give you more than that today?"

"Nope."

"Let me know if they do," Runnion told him as he rose and began heading toward the door. He glanced back as he left. Brady was waving the bill at the bartender with one hand and holding up two fingers of the other.

During McCurdy's early years on the streets—the period of his basic training in criminality, as it were—his partner was an older hood named Big Jim Larson, or Jimmy the Knife, as his associates affectionately called him. Larson had taught him a great many things, but McCurdy remembered one lesson above the others. The lesson was that you must work your way into a position of trust and loyalty with a man who will rise in the rackets. You obey him and never put any of his money in your pocket. These rules were not derived purely from loyalty but from enlightened self-interest and the history of crime and its practitioners. Violating them had cost many a man his life.

Following the rules allowed you to live, to remain close to the boss, and to profit in amounts far beyond what a guy like McCurdy could ever hope to make on his own, in or out of crime. A further consideration for adherence to the rules was that it put you in position for possible great rewards, if you were patient. As in the case of a major drug deal. Such a deal could allow one to become rich and go into business on one's own.

McCurdy had been thinking along those lines ever since Shapiro and he had started putting together the bits and pieces of Leo Baratto's travels and current whereabouts. Now they knew where Leo was, and that there were only a few places where he could have stashed the heroin. Mc-

Curdy wanted to be the only one who knew exactly where the dope was hidden. Acting on that desire, he returned to Baratto's apartment building to have another look around the super's apartment.

McCurdy thought there was a reasonable chance that the main chunk of heroin might well be in the super's residence. It certainly wasn't in Baratto's place—the cops would have found it. He realized that they had killed the super much too quickly, settling for the small bag of heroin he had told them about. They had accepted his statement that the hidden bag was all he had or knew about. Shit, McCurdy said to himself. We didn't even search the dump, come to think of it!

Had they not killed the super, they would have torn the place apart. But Shapiro had wanted him to get rid of the body quickly, and it had taken some doing to remove it and dump it in the empty field behind the airport. Frank didn't necessarily think the dope *was* in the apartment, but it might be. The possible reward was well worth the effort. He also wanted to look for anything at all that could give him some indication as to where the heroin could be found. If he could find it before Shapiro, he'd disappear so fast Shapiro would never get a line on his whereabouts. Wouldn't even know if he was alive. He didn't want to be Shapiro's flunky forever.

The area around the building was deserted, as were the halls of the building itself, as McCurdy stopped in front of the apartment door and surveyed the cheap lock. He had a small kit of burglar tools inside his coat, and he took out of it a little pry bar. In less than five seconds he had the lock popped and was closing the door behind him as he stood in the dark.

He propped a chair under the doorknob and quickly looked through the apartment to ensure that he was alone and that there were no surprises in store for him. He had once burglarized the home of a wealthy couple, who he knew were out for the evening. He also knew the housekeeper was asleep in an upper room. He felt completely safe in the house, alone with a housekeeper lost in dreamland. He knew where the alarms were, and where the wall safe was located; he had bought the combination from a maid who had spied on the owner. She had been fired by the owner's wife, who suspected that her husband was balling the girl. In her resentment, and over several drinks, she had confided in McCurdy.

McCurdy was walking toward the safe, a small flashlight in one hand and a .45-caliber pistol in the other, just in case. McCurdy was a believer in the hood's maxim that it is better to be caught with a gun than without one. Just as he was about to pocket the gun and begin working on the safe, his huge right foot came down squarely on the family cat, which let loose a bloodcurdling screech, which in turn caused McCurdy to shout and also involuntarily to jerk the gun and fire it, waking up the housekeeper, who immediately hit the alarm button, lighting up the entire house, indoors and out, and causing a piercing siren alarm to wail in the night. McCurdy was indeed fortunate to make a clean getaway that night, and ever since then he had looked over a place very carefully before proceeding with his business.

He noticed nothing different from his earlier time there. There wasn't much in the way of personal property or furniture. The super had not been a man who spent money, if he had it. McCurdy started with the small bedroom, realizing it is people's natural tendency to keep cherished objects close at hand. He dissected the dresser, drawer by drawer, looking into, under, and over every item. He tipped the entire dresser over, checking every nook and cranny. All he found in, under, or behind the dresser were dust and some old love letters addressed to the super. McCurdy thought it strange that any girl could like the ugly old bastard he had carried out of there.

He moved on to the bed and, after that, to the closet. He

found nothing out of the ordinary, only clothing items, shoes and shoe boxes, odds and ends. No heroin. No sign of a secret compartment. Now where? he wondered.

He decided to investigate the kitchen. There were decent hiding places in kitchens, he knew. In the refrigerator, his first stop, he found only two packages of raw hamburger. He went through the cabinets, looking into cereal boxes and bags of sugar, and checked for anything taped under the shelves. He tossed all the pots and pans out on the floor and checked under the table edge. Nothing. He went back into the living room and opened the closet where they had found the small bag of heroin. The guy had more old clothes than anyone he'd ever seen, even a moth-eaten raccoon coat. Must have never spent a dime on his clothes, McCurdy thought. So where the hell would a guy like that hide heroin, if he had any? He began pulling shirts and trousers off their hangers, searching their pockets, and dropping them on the floor. He found nothing of interest.

He sat down on the couch and looked over the box of junk where the super had told them the heroin was, just before Shapiro had cut his throat. He found a picture of seven men, with the words "Fire Team Alpha" written across its front. The super sure as hell hadn't been a soldier. He looked at the picture again. Yes, there was that little prick Baratto in the picture.

At first he was disappointed.

Then he realized that four of the soldiers in the picture had check marks on them. On the back of the picture were the names of the men, and four of them had lines drawn through them, leaving Baratto and two others. McCurdy studied the names. Two he didn't know, but Baratto, now, he knew exactly where *he* was at.

He sighed. Did that mean the dope was with one of those two remaining names? He smiled to himself. He would let Shapiro see the photo and decide the next move. The picture and the two strangers in it might mean something to Shapiro. He might get an idea of where to find the heroin. And when they found it, McCurdy decided, he'd take Shapiro out, too. He tucked the photo into his inside jacket pocket and left the building to find Shapiro and share the slim pickings from the caretaker's meager possessions.

6

It is an interesting fact about homicide cases that if there isn't a prime suspect found within the first few days of the investigation, along with a motive, the case usually gets buried under the rush of each succeeding day's accumulation of crimes. Every major police department has a large filing cabinet containing many unsolved cases, including murders.

A case will remain in that cabinet until some unexpected development renews an officer's interest in the "inactive but not closed" file. Policemen, especially detectives, want to investigate and solve every crime, to apprehend the guilty. However, reality often works on the side of the criminal and against the law. Time, manpower, and resources are the tools of police departments. Without sufficient tools, deserving cases are often set aside if there is no major lead to follow up. Each precinct has only so many officers and detectives, and not all of them are assigned to homicide.

Detectives usually work their asses off on murder cases, hating to have to put one in the "open" file unsolved. They *want* those cases solved. They dislike having a case solved by some rookie three weeks out of the police academy. After long and exhausting hours and much legwork, Lonto and Runnion were discouraged, disappointed, and disheveled. After this grueling day they needed to hear something pleasant. What they heard upon entering the station was both pleasant and unpleasant, it solved and unsolved the case. The desk sergeant was the first to speak.

"You guys can close the case on Baratto."

Lonto reacted first. "When was he picked up?"

"Someone made sure he *wouldn't* be picked up, except by an ambulance. Just got a call in from a patrolman on Vernon Avenue. Some kids found Baratto in a vacant lot over there. The officer made the identification from papers on the body."

"Shit. Goddamn!" Lonto said in a low, harsh voice.

"Did the officer mention anything unusual about the body?" Runnion asked.

"Oh, yeah. Guy had a wooden leg. Right one, I think."

"That sounds like our boy, Pat. When did you get the call, Sarge?"

"Oh, about fifteen minutes ago. Jaworski said to let you guys know as soon as you checked in. The lab boys and the coroner are on the way there."

Lonto and Runnion looked at each other as they turned toward the door, and Runnion said, "Looks like a long night, Tony."

"Yeah. It probably was long for Baratto, too."

Patrolman Sanchez was very cold and lonely for the first time in his life. He felt a bit nauseated and couldn't understand

114

why he was cold when the temperature in the lot had to be over a hundred. He kept stabbing at his forehead with a handkerchief now almost too wet to soak up another drop of perspiration.

He knew, of course, why he felt sick, and was thankful there were no other officers around to observe how finding his first corpse had affected him. The kids had told him there was a man in the weed-covered and rubble-filled lot. He had supposed it was some wino sleeping one off. It was a favorite place for area drunks, this lot, which had once held a factory.

He was greatly surprised by the corpse, noticing as he neared the body that there were an unusual number of flies flitting about the body. Before he reached the body he sensed that the man was not dead drunk, but just dead. As he stood over the body he saw the hands tied with a necktie and the blood matted into the man's hair. The sight, the odor of death, the flies, and the heat combined to send a surge of bile up his throat, while a wave of dizziness washed over him. He staggered back to regain his composure.

As his head and throat cleared, he noticed a wallet beside the body. As he rose to retrieve the wallet, a cloud of flies, protesting the interruption of their foraging, rose about him, creating, in their fury, the only breeze of the humid day. He recoiled from their dark and angry mass, as though thinking they might lay claim to him instead of the corpse.

He stepped a few feet away from the body, which lay on its side, its back toward him. He noted that the bonds were on both the wrists and elbows. The man's pants were torn and he could plainly see the cold plastic of the man's artificial leg. The man had obviously been the victim of a severe beating. His face was a mess, the eyes swollen shut, the nose crushed, the mouth a mass of red. Sanchez had moved away from the flies to call the station and returned to stand vigil over the body. He kept his distance from the body and stood still, hoping not to disturb the flies again.

Lonto and Runnion arrived just slightly after the coroner and lab technicians had begun their work. In this city and others, the investigating officers stay clear of a body until the professionals are finished. In this city, Isaac Frienberg was the coroner and chief medical examiner, and a tough, mean sonofabitch if he thought someone was interfering with his work in any fashion. It was the consensus among detectives that Frienberg solved more cases than any squad of detectives in town. He was tough, but he was damned good.

To have Frienberg support a theory with his work was the capstone of an investigator's case. No one ever said that sloppy work or unsupported conjecture of Frienberg's had lost a case or allowed the guilty to walk. A report issued by him was concise and complete, the facts presented in a manner that even the dumbest cop could follow to their conclusion. With his rank and stature, Frienberg could remain at his desk and send forth his assistants, but he chose to be present at as many homicide scenes as possible.

Frienberg was in a foul mood. He was used to the heat, but was working very tight-mouthed behind a handkerchief that he had to tie over most of his face to keep the flies off his skin and out of his mouth. "Jesus," he said, "this one would have been as ripe as shit if he'd been out here a couple more hours!"

Lonto stood slightly behind the ME, studying the scene as best he could as he peered over and around technicians. He didn't feel competent at this point to estimate the time of death; in fact, he was smart enough to know that only the experts could assess a murder victim's corpse with any precision. He knew, for instance, that heat could make a body appear to have been dead for a week. In this case he would bet even money that the beating, the heat, exposure, and the flies would make the time of death guesswork, even for the experts now examining the scene.

"Isaac, how long has he been dead?"

Frienberg peered up at Lonto over his shoulder, his eyes staring over the rims of his glasses. "I wouldn't even try to estimate this one, Tony. Not till I get him on the table. But I can tell you he hasn't been in this lot any longer than last night. He was dumped sometime after midnight."

"Is that an educated guess at this point, or something from your medical bag?" Runnion asked.

"That is right out of my textbooks." He grinned. "I happen to know how long it takes for fly eggs to hatch, and these here won't be hatching for several hours more. Nice to have caught him before the maggots started exercising."

"I'm sorry I asked," Runnion said.

"What do you think, Pat?" Lonto asked.

"I think we've got a new ball game. We're right back where we started, looking for a murder suspect."

Lonto nodded his agreement. "But I still think Baratto is our man in the Sullivan case."

"Or somebody who was tied in with the two of them."

"Like our friendly loan shark, knife man, pusher, and pimp, Shapiro?"

"None other," Runnion said.

"I doubt we can tie Sullivan in with that crew. Maybe we missed something, Pat. Maybe there's somebody else involved here. We've got two Nam vets murdered, maybe there's a connection there. These could even be revenge killings, with or without heroin involved."

"Maybe. But there's Shapiro, too."

Lonto glanced at his watch. "Yeah, there's always Shapiro when there's something down and dirty going on in this town. Maybe it's time we talked to him. Let's drop in and see how nervous he is. Isaac won't have anything for us until tomorrow anyway."

The two detectives smiled briefly at each other, relishing the prospect of trying to make Shapiro realize that his ass was close to the fire, and that they held the fire. They were

117

not unaware that the likelihood of getting anything solid from Shapiro or McCurdy was extremely slim. Both had long criminal records and were never known to have been broken under questioning. They were what was currently being called "career criminals."

But the case was going nowhere, and the detectives felt that they had to make *something* happen. Pressuring the two hoods just might make them silently apprehensive, might cause them to make a mistake somewhere down the line. When you're a cop asking questions about a murder case, you have a very powerful influence on those being questioned. Even an innocent man will squirm when he realizes he is a suspect in a murder investigation. So, too, will the guilty squirm, however well concealed that movement might be.

If the questioners have a few facts that tie the person being questioned into the web of things, even just a bit, that forces him to believe that the police might know even more than they have divulged. The thought arises that if they had found out about one thing, in some unknown manner, then what else could they have discovered?

A subtle threat mingled with the questioning is often effective. Force is always most effective when it is known to exist but is not flaunted. One's imagination works on the fear, and the very thought of what might happen is often more painful and effective than the force itself.

Lonto and Runnion were interested in how much of a surprise, if any, the news of Baratto's death would be to Shapiro and McCurdy. They wanted to see whether the two hoods would admit to any type of connection with Baratto.

They did not expect a warm welcome when they entered the combination tavern and pool hall on Forty-first and Silver. They weren't surprised. Nor were they surprised by the silence that descended upon the place at their entrance. It happened everywhere and anytime someone known or

118

thought to be a cop entered an establishment that catered to the shadow-dwellers in society. Immediate apprehension came upon every patron, followed by the question each asked of himself: Are they looking for *me*?

Shapiro was seated on a stool at his own bar, and McCurdy was standing behind it, wiping out shot glasses. The nickname Big Julie fit Shapiro like a glove. He was a mountainous mass of flesh when seated atop a bar stool. Sweating profusely, he peered at the detectives with tiny, bright eyes. "Well, well! Detective Lonto and his faithful Irish companion. To what do I owe this honor?"

"Detectives Lonto and Runnion," Lonto said, ignoring Shapiro's facetious opener. "Are you Julian Shapiro?"

Shapiro detected the cold undertone in Lonto's voice, and dropped his façade of jovial civility. "You bet your dago ass I am!"

"We'd like to talk with you and your pal McCurdy."

"What about? We're upright citizens and really can't think of any reason to talk to you."

"Shapiro, we can do this hard or easy, but we're going to do it. Make up your mind which way it's going to be."

"Listen, copper, we want to be left alone. Understand? If you don't have a warrant for me or Frank, fuck off. I don't have to talk to you."

"That goes for me too," McCurdy added.

"Answer a few questions, here or downtown, and you'll be left alone."

"What are you waiting for? Ask," Shapiro said, satisfied there was no warrant involved, and therefore nothing to worry about in talking to these assholes.

"Do you know a man named Leo Baratto?"

"Leo who?"

"Baratto," Lonto repeated. "The word on the street is that he's a good friend of yours. The word also says you miss him so much that you're paying big money to find him, and looking very hard yourself—probably so you won't have to pay for the information."

"How about that!" Shapiro said, grinning at the detectives and turning to McCurdy. "Do we know this guy, Frank? Name does ring a bell."

McCurdy showed them a smile that displayed his yellowing teeth. "Why are you guys after Leo?" he asked.

"You do know Baratto, then?" Runnion asked.

"Yeah. Sure. He's in and out of here a lot. Why are you looking for him?"

"Was he in here last night, at any time?" Lonto asked.

"No, he wasn't in here," Shapiro answered for McCurdy. "We haven't seen him around for several days now. Isn't that right, Frank?"

"Three or four days I think, boss."

"Are you certain of that?"

"Yes. Quite," Shapiro said. "Leo hasn't been in here lately, or in any of my other places."

"Is he a regular customer or a personal friend?" Lonto asked. "People say that Baratto is real close to you and McCurdy."

"Can't help what people say, can we? He's no friend of mine. His hanging around in here doesn't make him my pal. I just have a soft spot for crippled vets."

"It must be a real big soft spot, Julie," Runnion observed. "I hear you gave him a two-grand loan and were picking up his tabs all over town as well as paying his bills."

"I make no loans!" Shapiro said flatly. "All Baratto would get here is a drink or two on the cuff."

"Were you aware there was a warrant out on him?" Lonto asked.

"No shit?" Shapiro said. "Maybe you guys should be out there trying to find him, then, instead of hanging around here bothering us."

"We already know where he is," Lonto told him. "That's why we're interested in where he's been."

"Well, one place he hasn't been is in here. So what's with all the questions? You know where he's at."

Lonto glanced at Runnion, then looked Shapiro in the eye. "All of the questions are about first-degree murder, Shapiro. Baratto's dead and we hear he owed you money."

"I think you're full of shit, Lonto. Right up to your fucking ears. All Leo owed me was a few bucks in bar tabs."

"You didn't seem to be surprised to hear that he was murdered."

"Nothing surprises me," Shapiro said. "If he got himself hit in the head, that's his problem, not mine."

"Why don't you tell us exactly when you saw Leo last," Runnion suggested.

"We told you already. He hasn't been in here for a few days. And he owed only lightweight bar tabs."

"Sure," Lonto said.

"You bet," Runnion said, as both men stared at Shapiro.

"That's it," Shapiro said, after a minute of silence observed by all. "You guys want to ask me or Frank any more questions, you just take me to the station and you can talk to my lawyers."

"Do you think you need an attorney?" Lonto asked.

"We going to the station?" Shapiro asked in response.

Lonto smiled and let him wait for a moment or two. "Not today. But you and your partner there better keep your lawyers' numbers handy. We'll be back."

"Prick," Shapiro said behind them as they walked to the door.

Outside, the detectives paused near their car. Runnion was the first to speak. "Well, Tony?"

"My gut impression is that they're lying and that they knew Baratto was dead."

"I agree, but where does it leave us?"

They sat in the car and talked for several minutes and decided there was nothing more they could do until they had the coroner's report on Baratto's autopsy. They agreed also

121

that Baratto's getting himself killed was an inconsiderate pain in the ass. Then they went to the station to check out for the day.

The nice thing about being involved with a bank clerk, office worker, or construction worker, Robin thought, was that it would allow you to make plans and keep regular hours. You sent the man off on his nine-to-five and he was home by five-thirty with you and the kids, ready for the evening meal. A further advantage, she thought, was that those workers rarely came home with their work on their minds.

She was quickly realizing that a cop's job was always with him. And a cop like Tony Lonto spent a portion of his off-duty time thinking about his on-duty time. It was the sheep he worried over. He always characterized the people on the streets as a large flock of sheep being victimized by a small pack of wolves. She knew she would have to become accustomed to sharing him with the sheep he watched over. She knew they were a part of his life, part of his reason for living and caring. His *raison d'être*, as the French put it. His reason for being.

At odd moments she experienced a twinge of guilt over the manner in which she had pressured him into his marriage proposal. She had moved out on him, withdrawn somewhat, and given him the idea that she might remove herself completely from his life. In truth, she had no intention of attempting a life without him. But, she thought, smiling to herself, he doesn't need to know that, not now.

He was at that moment seated in an easy chair by the window, staring into the night. She knew his silence indicated that his mind was out there in the night, mulling over some nagging questions, reexamining clues. He had his feet up on the windowsill, the chair tilted back, his arms crossed over his chest.

She walked to him and stood beside him, waiting for him

to come off duty. She wore a flowered dress with nothing but a gold chain around her throat and tiny gold earrings, heart-shaped, exquisitely crafted. Her hair was tied back with a yellow ribbon. She stood there for several minutes before Lonto returned to her. He turned his head to his right and looked up at her.

"I'll bet you're trying to tell me something."

"Whatever gave you that idea? You were too far off to hear whatever you think I was trying to tell you."

"It's a case we're working on. But I guess you knew that."

"Want to share it with me?"

"It's a very brutal homicide case. The Sullivan case."

"The soldier?"

"Yes. The guy we were looking for, our best suspect, was also murdered. And his girlfriend is dead from an overdose. We think it was what is known as a 'hot shot'—that's a syringe full of acid or some kind of poison, or full of heroin in a strength great enough to kill. In her case, we don't think she knew what the spike held, in terms of potency. On top of that, there's a damned good possibility that there's a large amount of that super-strength heroin around, not yet on the street, but being held for the right deal or the right time to start selling it. The heroin is connected to the murders, and it shows up here and there in small amounts—at the murder scenes or at the homes of the murdered people. The lab told us they've never seen heroin this strong. The question is, how much is there and who has it?"

"Who do you think has it?"

"Now that Baratto's dead—that's our suspect—I think nobody has it; I think the bastard hid it or has someone keeping it. There are some very dangerous people looking for it, and I can't say they won't find it before we do. With what we know about the people, where would they keep it? Where is a safe place in town to stash millions of dollars worth of super dope? And I keep asking myself how they got it here to begin with."

Robin was puzzled. "You mean the soldiers?"

"Yes. If it is here, I think Sullivan and Baratto were the ones who brought it here—partners. They were in Vietnam together and I think they scored over there and somehow smuggled it over here—I don't know how, or what happened between then and now, when it started showing up."

Robin wiggled in his lap.

"Are you trying to distract me? I thought you wanted me to share this with you?"

"Who, me?" Robin asked innocently.

"Another question is what do you have on under this dress?"

"What happened to heroin and homicide?"

"That last little wiggle overdosed them."

Robin smiled impishly. "You mean the one where I moved like this?" she asked, with a twist of her hips.

"That's the one," he answered, his hand moving to cup a firm breast. "And the answer to my question is that you have absolutely nothing under this dress but flesh."

"I used to be a Girl Scout. You know the scout's motto, don't you? 'Be prepared.' One never knows who might drop in on one's last night in town."

"Like the mailman?"

Robin nodded.

7

For most of the city, Saturday was the first day of the weekend. For Lonto and Runnion, Saturday was their Friday. And when nearly everyone was enjoying Sunday, it was their Saturday. If you wanted to have a thoroughly confused calendar, you could be posted to a duty tour where your weekend fell on Wednesday and Thursday.

It wasn't that cops lived their lives by a special calendar that was days out of line with the rest of the world. It was simply that a cop shop couldn't close up every Friday night and reopen Monday morning. The bad guys worked a seven-day week, dictating the police department's scheduling. The cops and crooks worked odd hours.

It was one of the things that made Lonto wonder every now and then why he was still toting a badge and a gun.

After all, the job wasn't that damn great to start with. The hours sucked, he thought, and the risk factor was a constant, deeper shadow lurking in shadows—those in doorways, alleys, and the deep recesses of a cop's mind. To cap it off, the pay and politics were a pain in the ass, too.

The first time a cop wondered about this was when he first hit the street as a rookie in his shiny new uniform, his head full of thoughts of public service and the "war against crime," and illusions of being a Hero. It usually occurred that the bubble burst the same day, when some citizen he was protecting spit in his face and called him a "fucking pig." It dawned on him that when he was in uniform people looked at him differently, no matter how well or long they might have known him before he joined the force. He was shunned and viewed with suspicion and distrust, and it eventually drove him into the exclusive company of other cops, further isolating him from the real world.

He was no longer the guy from next door; now he was The Man, a threat, and immediately hated. He realized that he made people nervous, even his close pals.

The only time they wanted him was when some bastard was kicking their ass, stealing their car, or busting down their door in search of money, a TV, a piece of ass, or some other desired object. Yeah, it made Lonto wonder why. But deep inside he knew the answer, and it didn't always make him feel very good, or even much better than those he supposedly despised and sent to prison. The truth was that, just like the crooks, he needed the street life. It made him feel alive and gave meaning to his life. The danger and excitement, the high risks and flowing adrenaline, were as much a fix as any junky's shot of smack. There was only a very thin red line between crooks and cops; each needed the other. If all authority disappeared, crooks would go crazy; if crooks disappeared, cops would go just as nuts.

Like the crook around the next corner, Lonto detested

the life-style of the "normal" and "average" person, the deadly bore of early up, work, lunchbox, work, home, beer, TV, a three-minute fuck thrown into the old lady with all the genuine passion, love, and romance of a game of checkers, and then bed. And tomorrow, more of the same. Monotonous monotony. The mind-set was familiar to military shrinks at war's end, when they discovered, on both the winning and losing sides, that many soldiers did not want peace, that they wished the war would go on and on. They had never before lived at the peak of their emotions, never experienced the same sense of exhilaration as when they were involved in man's deadly games, and they never would again. Yes, he knew why he had become and now remained a cop.

And now, on this bright Saturday, neither he nor Runnion was snuggled up with a hot-blooded young thing; rather, they were engrossed with the herculean task, for them, of typing out reports on ancient machines in an attempt to defeat a growing mountain of paperwork stacked on each of their desks. Like most cops, they employed the schoolboy method of two-fingered, hunt-and-peck typing.

"Shit!" Runnion exploded. "These fucking foreign-made typewriters don't know how to spell in English."

"It isn't the machine, Pat. You're just a non-spelling, illiterate asshole," Lonto said with a grin. "By the way, did you send in that list of names—Baratto's army pals?"

"Yeah, with a copy of the photo. I asked for current addresses, jobs, and so forth for everyone. When we locate those guys, maybe they they can shed some light on Sullivan's and Baratto's activities in Nam."

"You know, Pat, it could be one of them is our man. One of them might be the real owner of the heroin."

"You don't think it will be that easy, do you?"

"No," Lonto replied. "But we need a break."

Isaac Frienberg didn't mind working weekends. As chief

medical examiner, and having spent many years on the job, he could delegate assistants to work the weekends while he stayed home with a good book and a bottle of bourbon. He could have Detective Hooley, for instance, handle the matter. He thought Hooley was a pretty fair medical examiner and lab man. He also thought Hooley was a bit too eager and ambitious and in need of restraint.

Frienberg liked working weekends when he didn't have Hooley underfoot and could work on a new homicide case by himself. Today he had Leo Baratto's body, which he would turn into several pages of facts, observations, and conclusions. His efforts might well result in the killer's apprehension. He was satisfied with his job and always satisfied by the detailed unraveling of the puzzles each victim's death presented for his solution.

Obviously, Baratto had not died of natural causes. It was clear to one and all that he had been quite deliberately murdered, beaten to death. Frienberg, however, never operated on the obvious assumptions. He was acutely aware that appearances were often misleading, and that the very precise cause of death could be the single most important element leading to the resolution of a homicide case. The exact cause of death was important to the police, to the district attorney, and to the potential defendant.

It could be, Frienberg knew, that Baratto had died of a heart attack suffered during the beating. This would make no difference to Baratto or the cops, but it could be the decisive factor in a defendant's being convicted of intentional, premeditated murder, or of being convicted of third-degree murder, homicide during the commission of a felony—the beating. The courts viewed things in that fashion. A judge would appreciate the difference between a finding of "death by beating" and "death by heart attack during a beating."

In Baratto's case, Frienberg learned that death had indeed resulted from several severe blows to the left side and rear of the victim's head. He did not doubt that the attacker had intended to kill Leo Baratto. Nor did he doubt that Baratto had suffered a long and systematic beating, lasting for several hours, prior to receiving the death blows.

Frienberg gave Baratto's clothing the same careful inspection his body had received. He examined the neckties used to bind Baratto's arms, the dirt under his nails, and a host of other factors. He made some preliminary conclusions: Baratto had not been able or in a position to defend himself, no struggle had occurred, and Baratto had in all probability been beaten in an apartment.

Frienberg spent several hours examining every conceivable possibility and clue. In most cases, most examiners perform a routine job, but Frienberg was painstakingly precise with every case. Although he was greatly experienced, he still felt a rush of excitement upon discovering some unknown or unexpected clue. Today was no different.

Isaac Frienberg was enormously pleased with himself, and decided that the detectives on this case should be told immediately of the rather brilliant work his lab had done. With a low-keyed whistle, he walked to the phone and dialed the River Station number of Tony Lonto.

"I was hoping to hear from you this morning, Isaac. Got anything for us?"

"You're always in a hurry, Lonto. Be more patient and precise and enjoy your work."

"Jaworski doesn't like it if we enjoy our work, and we don't have the time to be patient."

"Jaworski has ulcers from impatience."

"Where are you, Isaac, working? I thought Hooley would be the one to call."

"Hooley is doing his usual Saturday labor, chasing some stray skirts. I came in to handle the Baratto matter. I imagine you'd like the information I have?"

"Yes, Isaac. Your imagination is correct."

"The time of death was midnight Thursday, give or take no more than ten minutes in either direction—a twenty-minute time frame at most. Any one of three blows to the left side or back of the head killed him."

"Any idea of what he was smacked with?"

"I think he was beaten by a man who enjoyed his work and had great strength. The facial blows were by fists, but the killing blows were inflicted with a roundish, tubular object, probably a pipe or very similar object."

"Okay," Lonto said while he made notes.

"He was bound with neckties, two of them, very nice and expensive. According to the labels, they were from Sedwick's Men's Shoppe, that English-type place downtown."

"Well, that's something we can follow up on."

"Not much of interest with the rest of it, the negative aspects. No drugs in his system or clothing. If he carried dope in his clothes, he didn't spill any. He didn't need to use his clothes, anyway."

"Why not?" Lonto asked.

"Because everything he had of interest I found in his artificial leg, under the padding. This guy fits the jokes about people with hollow legs."

"What did you find, Isaac, and how much?"

"Only a few grams of heroin. But what's interesting is that he also kept a book stashed in there."

Lonto took a shot in the dark. "A Bible?"

"How did you know that?"

Lonto signaled Runnion to pick up the extension.

"His pal Sullivan has a sister. She told us about it."

"Wait a minute," Runnion interjected. "Wouldn't a Bible be too damn big to fit in that leg?"

"This Bible," Frienberg answered, "is a very soft leather book. He just rolled it up and it slid right into place. Is the Bible important?"

"It could be," Lonto replied. "The sister said it was important to Sullivan, but she didn't know why."

"It's obviously important to a blind man. It's in braille."

"We think there's more to it than that," Lonto said. "In any event, it must have some meaning or Baratto wouldn't have had it, let alone hid it in his leg. Have you examined it?"

"Of course," Frienberg said. "I've dusted it for prints and came up with a mess of smeared stuff. Other than that, there's nothing unusual about it."

"There has to be," Lonto countered.

"I only report what is there," Frienberg replied. "You guys are supposed to make sense out of it. There's nothing unusual about the Bible other than the text being in braille. There's nothing written or hidden in the Bible."

"That you can find," Runnion observed.

"Well, yes."

"It doesn't make sense," Lonto said. "Can you imagine a hood like Baratto carrying a Bible? On top of that, one he can't read? Even Sullivan was no Bible student."

"Well," Frienberg observed, "the world's full of nonsensical things. You want me to send the book over?"

"I guess so," Lonto said thoughtfully. "The damn thing fits into this case somehow."

"Well, I wanted to give you the information about the Bible, the cause and time of death, and to tell you that the heroin is from the same batch."

"Okay, Isaac. You haven't brightened up our day any. We have three bodies and they're all connected and we haven't found the connection."

"It's what you get paid for, Tony. Listen, I have some work to get at. Call me if I can answer any questions."

Interesting, Lonto thought. If there's no message in the Bible, why was it important, especially to Baratto? He smiled at their dilemma. Not just a mystery, but a mystery wrapped in braille.

"Talk to me," Runnion said, breaking into Lonto's musings.

"He might have made our day for us! It's an excuse to go see Faith Sullivan."

Runnion smiled in agreement. Being in an air-conditioned hotel room with a pretty girl beat the shit out of sitting at a typewriter in a hot-box office.

Faith Sullivan had taken a suite at the Riverview Hotel on Forty-second Street. She was wearing a white silk lounge outfit that could not hide the fact that beneath it she was naked. It was somewhat disturbing to grizzled cops unused to talking to beautiful young women in hotel suites. Her breasts kept getting in the way of their eyes.

"We're sorry to disturb your weekend," Lonto began after they had gone through the greetings and seatings. "But we have something we think you should see. Perhaps you can help us with our problem."

"Well, it's no disturbance. As you can see, I've just been loafing, and I appreciate the company. You two are the only people I know in town." She looked at the package Lonto had placed on the coffee table. "Is that what you want me to see?"

"It's your brother's Bible—we think," Lonto told her, holding it out to her.

"Where did you find it?" she asked, reaching for it.

"Leo Baratto had it. He's been murdered and it was in his artificial leg. Is it your brother's?"

"Yes." She pointed to a deep scratch in the cover. "That was there when he showed me the Bible in the hospital. Was there anything in it?"

"No," Lonto answered. "Can you recall anything specific that Walter told you about this Bible?"

"Only that it would be worth a lot of money to his partner. With Leo dead too, I don't know why it would be important now."

"Maybe this Bible is what got your brother and Baratto killed," Lonto said. "But we can't find anything in it."

"Perhaps you'll write and tell me if you find anything, and how the case finally turns out?"

"You're leaving?"

"Tomorrow evening. I've made all of the arrangements to take Wally home." She handed back the Bible. "There's nothing to keep me here any longer."

"I suppose not," Lonto agreed. "It hasn't been a pleasure trip for you."

"In a way, I'm glad it's over, all of it. Wally was never the same after the blindness. We were never what you call truly close, but we were the only family each other had."

Lonto stood, and Runnion followed his lead. "Call if we can be of assistance before you leave," Lonto told her as he reached for her hand. "And we will let you know how the case turns out."

She smiled at him as she shook his hand, holding it in both of hers. She turned to Runnion. "Mr. Runnion. It's been nice meeting you."

Runnion blushed and held out his hand. "Likewise for me, Faith. I'm sorry we met under these circumstances."

She led them to the door, giving each a final handshake as they said their goodbyes.

The man holding down the night-shift desk in Homicide at the River Station was Detective Peter Mills, the youngest man on the squad—which was why he was there on a Saturday night. His partner, Neil O'Malley, was out on the street playing detective and patting hookers on the ass. Saturday nights were busy for every cop shop in America, and Mills was holding his own with phones in each hand.

His assignment to Homicide didn't exempt him from other duties. On the desk job, he took incoming calls from citizens, and they could drive you bananas. Since he had sat down he'd taken reports on six burglaries and two muggings,

133

and there had been a rape report. At a quarter to midnight the phone rang again.

"Sixth Precinct. Detective Mills."

"I want to report a break-in," a voice said.

"May I have the location and your name and address?"

"I'm Charles Wolmer and the break-in is right next to St. Frances Church on Olson Avenue. In St. Frances Park."

"I'll try to get a car over there just as soon as I can, Mr. Wolmer. We're pretty busy tonight. A patrolman will contact you."

"I'll be at the church."

"Mr. Wolmer, it might be better if you stay at the scene until the car arrives."

"I'm not waiting in a graveyard for a cop car!"

"Are you telling me it's the cemetery that's been broken into?" Mills asked incredulously.

"Yeah. St. Frances Cemetery."

"Are you serious, Mr. Wolmer? This isn't a gag?"

"Listen. Somebody broke in and dug up a grave and the body is out on the grass!"

"Mr. Wolmer, stay right there! I'll get a car there in a few minutes. You stay there and keep cool." Mills hung up and turned to the dispatch panel and picked up the mike. He ordered the nearest patrol or detective squad in the area to the scene. No car could take the call, they were all tied up. Mills ordered a patrolman from the lockup area to handle the phones, and he ran to his car and sped to the cemetery alone.

Sooner or later every cop in a big city is exposed to practically every crime known to man, which explains why very little surprises policemen. But even long-time veterans do not experience grave-robbing except on the "Late, Late Show." Mills was of course surprised at the sight of the open grave, the open coffin, and the long-dead body draped on top of it. He was also disturbed by the crime, which presented an obvious problem: there was a ghoul on the loose. He stood there looking over the scene, trying to imagine what reason the perpetrator had for this offense. He would have assumed robbery if the grave had been fresh; some people are buried wearing a great deal of expensive jewelry.

Mills went closer and looked at the tombstone. The man had been dead for seven years. The odor of death crept up out of the grave and probed his nostrils. He quickly stepped back from the open wound in the earth. He wondered just what he should do, whom he should call. What was this, a burglary, breaking and entering, vandalism? He racked his brain and recalled that departmental regulations stipulated that all bodies discovered under unusual circumstances must be reported to the Homicide Division. Mills wrote down the pertinent information he already knew, and the information on the tombstone. He went to the car and radioed the precinct commander, the duty officer, and Lieutenant Jaworski. Then he notified the coroner's office, the lab, and the police chaplain, because he figured there'd be some sort of religious involvement and because he knew that his colleagues weren't simply going to come here and stuff the body back into the grave. It was going to require some special attention to answer the many questions the incident would raise. Mills knew he'd have a long Saturday night.

The following morning, Lonto and Runnion found Mills asleep in a swivel chair in the back of the squad room. It wasn't unusual following a Saturday night, in the quiet hour before the morning shift came in. That shift always came in early to check the previous night's logs and reports, compare notes with the departing detectives, and clear up any last-minute paperwork they had put off. This Sunday morning found Jaworski on the scene, in his usual ill humor.

"I thought I'd take a few minutes of your time to congratulate you boys! Not only have you two master investigators

135

managed to solve a case by having the prime suspect turn up murdered himself, but this guy"—Jaworski pointed at Detective Mills, momentarily forgetting his name—"Mills, he wakes me up at midnight to report he has a corpse who woke up and crawled out of his grave. A seven-year-old corpse he just couldn't wait a few more hours to tell me about."

"The manual says to treat any body as a potential homicide matter," Mills said defensively. "It's in the book."

"Yeah, yeah. I know," Jaworski waved him to silence. "Any body found under unusual circumstances. And I gotta agree with you, Miles, the circumstances were unusual."

"Yes, sir. Sir, it's Mills."

"What?"

"Mills, sir. You called me Miles."

"Yeah, Mills. I know your damn name! I expect my men to follow procedures, Mills. But I also expect you to exercise some discretion and common sense. It was not, however, a matter of sufficient urgency to wake up half the fucking brass in town!"

"I thought I was doing my duty, Lieutenant."

"Yeah. Look, Miles, I really think you did fine. Sorry if I sounded upset. Just next time call only the duty officer."

"Yes, Lieutenant."

"Now what about this case? Is it some kids fucking off, a pre-Halloween prank?"

"We're working on it now, sir," Mills said. "We're seeing the family to find out if the dead man, Arlen Nimlos, was buried with valuables. That doesn't appear likely, though."

"Why not?" Jaworski wanted to know.

"Frienberg told me that it's pretty rare for people to be buried with really valuable stuff nowadays. It's all removed before the casket is sealed."

Runnion was flipping noisily through his notebook. When he found the sought-after entry, he held it out to Lonto to read as Jaworski watched them.

"Would you ace detectives like to add something to this discussion, or aren't you interested in police business?"

"What was the man's name again, Mills?" Lonto asked, ignoring Jaworski's comment.

"Arlen Nimlos. Why?"

"Arlen Nimlos is one of Leo Baratto's and Walter Sullivan's army buddies from Vietnam. If it's the same guy. With a name like that, it's possible! What was the date of death?"

"June Nineteen Seventy-two."

"Before the war was over," Lonto said thoughtfully. "Anyone find out if he was killed in Asia, or if he died after he got home?"

"Not yet. There's a connection between this guy and Leo Baratto, those killings?" Mills asked.

"Maybe there's no connection at all. But he might be one of their pals, and lately every murder case we've had has been connected to Baratto and Sullivan. I wonder why."

"Why don't you and Runnion find out?" Jaworski asked. "You two check it all out, Lonto. And if this Nimlos is connected to the other case, then you've got this case too. And I want some fucking action and results pretty soon! Have you got anything on Baratto's murder?"

"Not much," Lonto replied. "Street rumors connecting him to Shapiro and McCurdy, loan-sharking and heroin. Same stuff we've been hearing."

"Then get some hard facts. Force a break in this log jam. We've got a regular daisy chain here, from one body to the next! Now we got a corpse coming up like this was a fucking zombie movie. You've worked your stoolies, I assume?"

"We've worked everything, Lieutenant," Runnion said. "One of mine gave me the tip on Baratto being into the sharks pretty heavy."

"Well, start leaning on the stoolies. These cases are drawing the attention of the boys downtown, including the commissioner. I don't like that bastard to begin with, and it pisses me off having to answer his questions with no answers. What about you, Lonto?"

"Word is that Baratto was involved with or trying to get involved with a big heroin deal. The lab reports that the smack that has turned up is the highest quality they've ever seen. We don't know yet if there's enough of it around to get worried about."

"Well, get out there and get something moving on this shit. If this corpse is connected to Baratto and whatever he was hooked up in, we want to know fast. Miles here won't mind if you take this case. I want hard facts, today. Got it?"

"Yes, sir," Lonto and Runnion replied in unison. They turned and left the squad room.

"Why are you still here, Miles? Your shift is over."

"Yes, Lieutenant. I'm leaving," Mills replied, biting back his impulse to tell Jaworski his name again.

Lonto and Runnion stopped at the front desk before they went to their car. "Any calls for us, Sarge? We're expecting some information from army records."

"On Sunday? Are you nuts, Lonto? Take it from me, kid—the fucking army don't work on no Sunday. And it's usually off the rest of the week."

"Yeah, I guess you're right," Lonto said, and turned toward the door leading to the garage, pulling Runnion along with him.

"Hey, you two!" Sergeant Wolverton called after them. "Did Jaworski leave you guys with any ass?"

As the two detectives neared the door, Lonto lifted the back of his suit coat and gave Wolverton an answer to his question.

8

It was all going too easy—even for Sunday, when a man's day is supposed to go well. Lonto and Runnion stopped at St. Frances Church on Olson Avenue, where they were greeted by the parish priest.

"Father, I'm Tony Lonto and this is Pat Runnion. We're with the police and investigating the incident concerning the Nimlos grave last night."

"Well, good morning, officers. I guess in addition to the bearers of God's law, the bearers of man's law also busy themselves on His day. I'm Father John Vernon. Come with me into the rectory. We can be more comfortable there. If you drink on duty," he added with a smile, "perhaps you'll join me in a bit of fresh lemonade."

"You must have seen *The Godfather*. That's an offer we can't refuse," Lonto told the priest. They walked toward the rectory with the priest between them.

"Now," Father Vernon said, after he had poured three glasses of lemonade and seated the detectives and himself. "How can I help you with this ghastly business?"

"Father," Lonto began, "were you acquainted with Arlen Nimlos?"

"Why, heavens, yes! I've known the whole family for many years. His parents are still members of this parish."

"If you would be so kind to give us their address, Father? We must talk with them."

"Certainly. I have it on my desk. Mr. Runnion, would you be so kind to reach there and pass it to me? Yes, the red leather notebook. Thank you." The priest thumbed a few pages and read the address to Lonto.

"Father. What do you think happened last night?"

"Well, I'm assuming it was simply some terrible sort of prank. Perhaps some of the more unruly kids in the area."

"There's a possibility it was more than that."

"Why do you say that, Mr. Lonto?"

"It appears that Nimlos was probably connected in some fashion to some drug-related murders."

"Hmm." Father Vernon held his chin in his right hand. "I felt perhaps there was more to it than simple vandalism."

"Why do you say that, Father?"

"Well, most people have an inherent fear of disturbing the dead. You know, the old childhood boogeyman sort of stuff. Even if we watch horror movies now and laugh at our childhood nightmares, there's still a trace of that time left in each of us, I suspect.

"A vandal, even a bunch of kids, might tip over a tombstone or two—that's happened every now and then. Some write graffiti on the stones. But actually digging up a coffin and opening it—not to mention taking the body out! I just can't imagine anyone doing that without a better reason than vandalism or prankishness."

"Nothing more specific, Father?"

"Oh, no. It's just the incongruousness of it."

They finished off their drinks and thanked the priest, who talked them both into a donation for the collection being taken up for reburial services for Arlen Nimlos.

The Nimlos home was in the St. Frances Park section of town, some three miles from the church. The detectives arrived at ten-thirty, pulled into a tree-lined drive, and parked behind a blue van. The homes in this area were mostly single-family residences with large yards and painted fences. The home they were visiting had been recently painted, white with blue trim. A neatly lettered sign on the porch read D. NIMLOS.

Lonto and Runnion mounted the steps and Lonto rang the bell. In perhaps half a minute, a small, gray-haired woman opened the door and said, "Yes?"

After a quick smile and a nod of his head, Lonto answered her question. "Good afternoon, ma'am. I'm Detective Lonto and this is Detective Runnion. Might we have a few minutes of your time?"

"Yes, officers, please come in. Father Vernon spoke to me of you earlier. Sit down, gentlemen."

She took a seat across from them in the spacious, cool living room. She looked sorrowful as the three of them talked about the previous night's events. Mrs. Nimlos simply did not understand what had happened. She was at a loss for any possible reason or motive. It had been most painful and heartbreaking to bring her son home from that awful war, to bury him. Now she would be forced to go through it all again. She had just completed the arrangements shortly before Lonto and Runnion arrived.

"We lost him in that senseless war," she told them. "Now I have to bury him again after another senseless act."

"We understand your sorrow, Mrs. Nimlos. We won't impose too much on your time and privacy," Lonto said to her. "Father Vernon told us that Arlen's funeral was a closed-casket service and that there were no personal effects interred with him. Is that accurate, ma'am?"

"The casket was never opened. The body was in one of those awful bags the army provided, and they sealed it in Vietnam. Arlen's property was sent to us separately."

Runnion held out his open notebook to her and asked, "Ma'am, do you recognize any of these men besides your son?"

She studied the names for several moments and then returned the book. "Derrick Kinder was a friend of Arlen's. They served together."

"Do you know where he is?"

"He lives in the city. I met him just once."

"When was that, Mrs. Nimlos?"

"At the funeral. He was the only one in uniform."

"Did Arlen ever mention him in letters?"

"No, I never heard of him. He introduced himself at the funeral. He told me that he had served with Arlen and had just returned from Vietnam. He was quite a nice boy."

"But you don't know where we could find him?"

"No, I'm sorry. Even if he told me, I've completely forgotten."

"Very well, ma'am. It was nice meeting you, and we'd like to express the police department's condolences."

"Thank you, Mr. Lonto," she replied, leading them to the door, where she shook hands with both detectives and watched them walk to their car.

"Well?" said Lonto as they pulled away from the Nimlos home.

"We'll run Kinder through the mill and see what we can find. I won't be surprised if it turns up zero—after . . . what? Seven years?"

"He's a possible suspect, Pat. Shit! Every name in your book is a suspect."

"Don't forget Humpty and Dumpty—Shapiro and his ape."

"I haven't forgotten. But we need something solid to connect them."

"Maybe we should pull them in on any of the shit they run over there, the whores, the gambling?"

"Their lawyers would have them out in five minutes and they wouldn't tell us diddly-shit."

Runnion grinned. "Maybe not. But we could yank their asses in and search their homes before we book them. We could come up with something to hold them on, and then sweat them both."

"Well . . ." Lonto ran the idea around in his mind. "If we could get Judge Larson to give us a warrant, we could make those bastards sweat bullets. But we better find something, or Larson will roast our asses!"

"Yeah, but Jaworski's gonna burn us if we don't make a move. Remember? 'Break the log jam.'"

"What or who can we use to swear out a warrant?" Lonto asked.

"My boy. Bootleg Brady. He'd swear to the loan-sharking."

"You don't think Bootleg sort of represents a very weak probable cause? The man is a raving wino!"

"What else have we got?" Runnion complained. "Do we care if Shapiro and McCurdy scream about police harassment? Or the heat?"

They thought about it and grinned simultaneously.

"Let's do it!" Lonto said. "You go get the warrant while I look up an old friend."

"Who?"

"Blind Jimmy. We have a book for him to read, right?"

They drove back to the station together, agreeing to meet there later and go for a late lunch. On his way to the courthouse, Runnion gave little thought to the matter of the warrant; he was more concerned about Blind Jimmy reading the Bible—and possibly finding something they could use. He and Lonto knew they were beginning to look like Keystone Kops on this case; they both resented the appearance. He himself didn't like the approach they had been forced to employ so far. All they were doing was stirring up the shit and hoping a rat would emerge and come their way.

He knew that Shapiro and McCurdy were simply too experienced and too well versed in crime and law to have made a fatal error. But this long shot with the search warrant might just wind up as a lucky stroke. Maybe the two hoods were so cocksure of themselves that they had made errors, and evidence might turn up in their homes. It was worth a try.

He began thinking of his immediate problem. One simply doesn't ask a judge to interrupt his Sunday and come to the courthouse to issue a search warrant without something fairly solid. Runnion had to swear that he had reliable information regarding some criminal offense. The law allowed him, at this point in a legal proceeding, not to disclose the source of his information, to name Bootleg.

He felt reasonably sure that Judge Larson would not hassle him. He had a good rep as a cop, and the two targets were infamous city gangsters whom, Runnion knew, Judge Larson disliked personally, as well as for their alleged criminal enterprises.

It took less than an hour, and Runnion was on his way back to the station with the warrant in hand.

Julian Shapiro had a history of accepting calculated risks in his daily life. He believed that life itself was nothing but a calculated risk. He also believed that he was destined to be one of those who plucked the millions of pigeons with money in hand and vice in heart. He sat now, high and comfortable, on his specially built bar stool in the pool hall. He was basking in the knowledge that very soon he would be immensely wealthy, and he was trying to think of someone who might deserve it more than he.

It was now all his. The Baratto-Sullivan duo were dead,

and he had it all. Millions of dollars would be his alone. Except that he expected McCurdy to demand a larger— much larger—piece than he planned to offer; or he might even be thinking about taking it all. That could be handled in due course, Shapiro realized. He didn't need McCurdy, not if he was going to live the life of a multimillionaire. In fact, now that everyone connected to his pot of gold was safely dead, it was only logical that McCurdy would join them in eternal repose. Certainly McCurdy couldn't travel with him; he would be out of place in the South of France, London, and the other places Shapiro intended to travel to, alone—except for some real nice broad. Shapiro's mind was awhirl with visions of sugar plums.

Policemen are notorious for disturbing happy thoughts. Lonto and Runnion did not fail to uphold that tradition. At one-thirty that Sunday afternoon they turned up at the pool hall. They came in their car, accompanied by a police van with six patrolman in it. They also came with the nice new search warrant. Their very first move was forcefully to hustle Shapiro and McCurdy into the back of the van. Second, they chased everyone out of the pool hall, two of the patrolmen lining them up outside and questioning them thoroughly.

Lonto and Runnion would also question them, before getting to the main two. It was only when the questioning began that Shapiro and McCurdy would be entitled to have their attorneys notified. Before they ever talked to them, the police would spend as much time as possible in a very thorough search. Another team was at Shapiro's home and yet another at McCurdy's apartment.

The three searches took exactly seven hours. Nothing remotely incriminating was discovered anywhere.

9

Sy Rosenberg, Shapiro's attorney, arrived at the River Station within twenty minutes of receiving Shapiro's call. He immediately demanded of the police that they verify that they had informed his client of his rights. Lonto assured him in no uncertain terms. Rosenberg then demanded to know what the charge was.

"At this time we're not contemplating filing any charges, but we want to question them regarding Leo Baratto and their relationship with him," Runnion answered.

"Are you representing McCurdy, too?" Lonto asked.

"Yes," Rosenberg told him. "Are you planning on questioning them both at once?"

"We're looking for information, not booking them."

"Then I have no objections to the questioning. Where are they?"

146

"Bring them in, Pat," Lonto said, eyeing the suave and well-dressed attorney. He took in the suntan, the light gray hair at the temples, the expensive suit, and the sharp black eyes.

Runnion returned with Shapiro and McCurdy. Shapiro did not look very pleased to be there. McCurdy was harder to read. "Hello, Sy. Glad you could come," Shapiro said.

"Okay, gentlemen. Let's all be seated and start with the full names and addresses of the suspects."

"Look, Lonto," Shapiro said, "you've got all sorts of that shit on file from the other times you ran us in. If we're going to talk, let's talk, and fuck this petty bullshit!"

"All right, Shapiro. We'll do it your way. What do you own and operate besides the bar and pool hall?"

"Nothing."

"No massage parlors?"

"Nothing but the bar and pool hall."

"Was Leo Baratto involved with either of you in any sort of business, legal or illegal?"

"He came to the bar and bought booze. He was a customer and nothing more."

"That's your view too, Frank?"

"Yeah. Just a customer."

"No friendship with either of you?"

"Wait a minute," Rosenberg interjected. "If you're interested in general information, why are you trying to establish a relationship between this Baratto and my clients?"

"We want to know why Baratto spent so much time in that particular tavern. It couldn't have been the clean and wholesome atmosphere."

"Well, go ahead, then," Rosenberg said grudgingly.

"All right," Lonto began again. "Baratto spent an awful lot of time there. Are you saying that neither of you had a friendly relationship with him, beyond his being a customer?"

"Listen, Lonto," Shapiro replied, "the guy was a pure juicehead and he hung around because we'd give him a little credit. Around the end of the month, we'd carry him until he received his government check."

"Then you loaned him money?"

"A bar tab is hardly a loan, Lonto," Rosenberg observed.

"Perhaps not. Did you ever loan money to him or to anyone else?"

"I run a fucking bar, not a loan office!"

"How many customers receive the treatment you gave to Baratto?"

"A few regulars. Guys we know will pay up."

"How much credit did you give Baratto?"

"I really don't know, Lonto," Shapiro replied. He turned to McCurdy. "Did you keep the tab, Frank?"

"No. The bartenders ran it. None of those tabs run more than fifteen, maybe twenty bucks."

"Nowhere near a grand or two?" Runnion asked Shapiro.

"Fuck, no!"

"How well did you know him?" Lonto asked.

"Who gets to know a drunk?"

"You never talked with him during the few years he was coming into your place?"

"Yeah," Shapiro said. "We shot the shit now and then."

"What about?"

"Well, he talked about Vietnam a lot. To hear him tell it, he won the war singlehanded, which I thought was strange, 'cause everyone else thinks we lost it." Shapiro laughed at his own observation. "He bragged a lot."

"That's right," McCurdy chimed in.

"About the army?" Lonto asked.

Shapiro glanced at McCurdy, then turned his attention back to Lonto. "The army, or the war?" he asked Lonto.

"The army, and his pals over there. He must have talked about the guys he served with. Right?"

"Yeah, maybe he did. But I never paid any attention to it if he did. You hear him talk about his buddies, Frank?"

McCurdy shook his head and lit a cigarette.

"Did Baratto ever offer to sell you anything or cut you in on any deals?"

"Sell me what? His fucking wooden leg?"

"Is that what you loaned him the two grand on, his leg?"

"I never loaned him two Gs or anything else. Bar tabs, just bar tabs."

"Who *do* you loan money to?"

Shapiro turned to Rosenberg. "These assholes are trying to weave a loan-sharking case on us, Sy!"

"Is that what you're up to, Detective?"

"Mr. Rosenberg, the only person to mention loan-sharking has been your client. Are you objecting to the questions so far?"

"I'd like to know where you're going with this line of questioning. If you're trying to connect these men to a murder through an alleged loan, I think this has gone far enough. I would have to advise them not to answer any further questions along those lines."

"Mr. Rosenberg," Lonto countered, "we have information that your two clients loaned Baratto two thousand dollars shortly before he was murdered."

"What is your source?"

Lonto smiled. "Confidential, counselor."

"Why? If you're not pressing charges, why is the source secret? Or *are* you pressing charges?"

"Not right now," Lonto said. "We have reason to believe, as I indicated, that your clients loaned Baratto two grand as part of an anticipated drug deal between them."

"Presumably," Rosenberg replied, "this is all hearsay, or you'd not be on this fishing trip and trying to intimidate my clients. I'll ask you this, Detective. Do you have specific, concrete evidence that my clients are or were involved in a crime, and do you intend to file charges?"

"We have enough reasonable and probable cause to hold them for questioning."

"I assume you realize, Mr. Lonto, that this interrogation is now over, and that I'll have my clients out of here inside half an hour?"

"Look, counselor, your clients are mixed up in this drug matter, right up to their pointy little heads! And we'll pull them in every week until we get something to stick!"

"That sounds like a threat of harassment. Are you going to charge them or not?"

"I really don't know yet," Lonto said.

"All right. I suggest that you do charge them. Right now. They've been held here for quite a while already without a charge. I insist that you charge and book them now. Or let them go. *Now*."

"We're aware of the legal aspects, counselor," Runnion told the lawyer. He glanced at Lonto, who shook his head.

"Well?" Rosenberg asked impatiently.

"Let them go, Pat. We'll charge them later, when it will stick like the smell of shit."

"That'll never happen, cop," Shapiro informed him.

They spent a very glum half hour following the departure of the lawyer and his two clients. It had been a very unprofitable exercise. And frustrating. Being a cop wasn't easy. It was always especially painful to know when you had a guilty party but simply couldn't prove it. The law you swore to uphold dictated specific rules for you to follow; too often these rules hampered the very practice of the law, in enforcement and judicial proceedings. But that went with the territory.

Lonto and Runnion were drinking coffee when the duty officer provided proof that the U.S. Army indeed worked on Sunday. They received an address for Corporal Derrick Kinder.

The address, on East Willow, in Maple Hills, had been entered on the army records four years before. It didn't show much promise that Kinder still lived there. But Kinder was a possible suspect, and the two detectives checked out and, off duty, went to the address. Kinder appeared to be the sole surviving member of the group of GI pals.

They rehashed what they knew on the way to Maple Hills. The murder victims were all connected to the heroin. It appeared that there could be a hefty amount of the drug in town. None of it had yet hit the streets. Whoever had it must be hiding it, making a deal to dump it in one transaction. Or, of course, it might not be in anyone's possession.

Kinder still lived at the address the army had given them. It was an apartment on the third floor of a singles-only building. It was an affluent man's apartment, entirely masculine in appearance.

"Sure," Kinder informed them. "I know everyone on that list." He settled down into a reclining chair. He was in his late thirties, with the well-conditioned body of an athlete but with a weathered face. "Most of those guys were snuffed in Nam."

"Have you kept in touch with those who came back home?" Lonto asked him.

"Me? No! I was discharged and felt no connection to anything or anyone from over there. I was out and didn't need any kind of reminders. What's this all about, anyway?"

"We're investigating the backgrounds of Walter Sullivan and Leo Baratto. Remember them?"

"Sure. The Sarge and Fuck-Up. I've hardly thought of them in years."

"Did you know they lived in this city?"

"The only one I knew about was Arlen Nimlos. I went to his funeral. Are the Sarge and the Fuck-Up in trouble?"

"They were both murdered, Mr. Kinder. That's why we're interested in their old friends."

"No shit! They were murdered?" Kinder sounded amazed.

"No shit," Lonto assured him. "Can you think of anyone known to you and them who might have wanted to see them dead?"

"Christ, no! Shit, you're talking, what, seven, eight years ago? I haven't seen any of that crew since Nam. I wouldn't have any idea," he said, lighting a cigarette.

"Someone on the fire team, perhaps?" Runnion suggested.

"Not really. No one liked Baratto very much, but no one disliked him enough to follow him home and whack him! I mean, shit, if you wanted to kill them, Nam was the perfect place to do it and get away with it!"

"Perhaps the killer's reason surfaced later, here, now? How did you get along with them?"

"The Sarge and I were pretty cool. Baratto was a sneaky little cocksucker. I stayed clear of him."

"Any particular reason?"

Kinder shrugged. "I always suspected he was one of the dope pushers over there—to our guys. Lots of kids OD'ed in Nam. I didn't like the motherfucker."

"Then the last time you saw either one was in Vietnam?"

"That's right," Kinder said. "In Nam. I haven't seen any of that bunch back in the States."

"That was seven or eight years ago?"

"Yeah, around there."

"Mr. Kinder," Runnion said, "if you were required to account for your whereabouts during the past week, could you do so?"

"What—an alibi?"

"Basically."

"For when?"

"How about last Sunday night?"

"That's easy!" Kinder exclaimed. "I know exactly where

I was. Right down the hall with Carol, as usual. In fact, we spent the weekend together."

"We'll check with her. Just a couple more questions. You said Baratto was pushing in Nam. I understand heroin was easy to get."

"Man, you could get anything there! As much as you wanted."

"How difficult would it have been for a GI to bring a nice piece of smack back to the States? For Baratto to do it?"

"Well, I never gave it much thought, but I know they never checked us out very well, not when I rotated back here. I suppose it could be done. But they did do sneaky, random inspections."

Lonto looked at him, deep in thought. "What if he wanted to bring back a big piece? Could it be done?"

"How big?"

"A pound. Two. Maybe more."

"That would be a pretty big bundle, man. You can't carry something like that off the plane. Not easily."

"How about a cigar box or two in size? Could you get it off the ship with no hassle?"

"Is that what Baratto did?"

"We don't know. It's possible. And it could be the cause of his death. Sullivan's, too."

"Well, if he had some help," Kinder offered, "he could have shipped stuff back here. Depends on his connections. I heard over there that some guys were shipping souvenirs back—shit they ripped off Charlie and couldn't keep, legally. The word was they were doing it through the meat house."

"What is the meat house?" Lonto asked.

"That's the name we gave the unit that received the dead soldiers and took care of shipping them home—put 'em in the boxes and on the planes."

Lonto stood and began pacing. "I understand from Mrs.

153

Nimlos that the body bags were sealed over there and never opened. All a guy would need to know was the name of the corpse and where it was being shipped to."

"Yeah," Kinder said. "But, listen. I don't know that anything like that went down, you know? I couldn't testify to any of this."

They assured him he had nothing to concern himself about. They weren't interested in how it was smuggled. They believed they knew where the heroin had been kept all along. They asked Kinder several more questions, were satisfied he was clean, and then left.

Sometimes it takes only a tiny scrap of information to make a case come together. They believed it had come together for them now. Lonto voiced it first.

"Two guys decide to let the army help them become rich. Leo has the connections over there and connections here. And our hero soldier, Walter Sullivan, apparently has the connections over there to get the stuff shipped back in the coffin of our wandering corpse of last night, Arlen Nimlos."

"That explains why the two of them, so different, were together," Runnion offered.

"And Sullivan, knowing that Baratto was a sneaky little bastard, kept the vital information to himself. And I bet it was in the Bible, the name of Arlen Nimlos and where he was buried."

"What do you think happened, Tony? Between Baratto and Sullivan?"

"The war. They didn't plan on getting shot to shit. Leo laid around getting nervous and broke, broke and nervous, and went to Shapiro and told him the whole deal—what he knew."

"And they waited till Sullivan was able to leave the VA?"

"Yeah. And then murdered him to get the information as to which grave the smack was in."

"And then Shapiro iced Baratto?"

"Naturally. That bastard wouldn't deal straight with a no-body like Baratto. But I have a hunch Baratto didn't know the whole score. I think there's a chunk of smack out there that we'd better locate fast."

"We can't—are you thinking of another grave? Whose?"

Lonto told him his thinking. They discussed it and went to share their idea with Lieutenant Jaworski.

10

Monday is everybody's blues day. The start of another long, dull work week. An August Monday is the worst. And on this Monday, to start it off in conference with Jaworski was even worse.

There comes a point in each case when you have to demonstrate why they gave you a gold shield and left the lower-ranked detectives with their silver badges. It didn't require a Holmesian analysis, necessarily, but all logical deduction follows Sherlock's method to some extent. Holmes believed that when you have eliminated the possible, then whatever is left, however improbable it might be, is the answer.

Lonto and Runnion sat before Jaworski and began telling him how they had come to perceive the case. Lonto spoke, as senior man of the two, and as the author of the idea.

"We see it like this, sir. Sullivan and Baratto set up a very sweet and uncomplicated drug deal in Vietnam. Baratto was a hood, and Sullivan had always had daydreams of being a rancher.

"The Vietcong complicated the picture by whacking off Baratto's leg and blinding Sullivan. Sullivan had the key information, and with the two of them back home, hospitalized, they had to delay completing their scheme. No problem, they're not in shape yet to go off to Europe and play the casinos.

"After waiting as patiently as he could for Sullivan to get well and get out of the hospital, Leo gets him where he can start asking questions—like, where the hell is the dope? Sullivan tells him to get fucked. Leo tortures him, Sullivan dies. Maybe he told Leo something before he died. In any event, Leo's running scared. He tells Shapiro about the dope and gets a loan pending delivery of the smack. Now he has killed the golden goose before the egg is laid.

"Leo is wanted by us. He crawls into a hole with some junky hooker and appeals to Shapiro's better nature and tells him what he knows, including the location of the smack, which he has given them samples of before this. That was the kicker for Shapiro—he loaned him two grand.

"Shapiro found Leo before we did. They got from him whatever he had and killed him. Now there's no one else to share the smack and the money with. We think it's Shapiro and McCurdy who dug up the Nimlos grave, and that they are going to dig up the graves of every man who was a part of Sullivan's Fire Team Alpha. We've either got to find it first or bust them with it."

Jaworski listened carefully, head cocked to one side as he shifted his gaze from one to the other. "Let's see that list of names."

Runnion opened his notebook and passed it to the lieutenant.

1. Sgt. Walter Sullivan (murdered)
2. Cpl. Derrick Kinder (alive, local resident)
3. Cpl. Arlen Nimlos (killed in VN—grave robbed)
4. Pfc. Asa Crain
5. Pfc. Albert Beall
6. Pvt. Virgil C. Staffer
7. Pvt. Leo Baratto (murdered)

"What about Crain, Beall, and Staffer?" Jaworski asked.

"We're still waiting on army records. They were all listed as killed in action, but we don't have the dates and where they were shipped to. Whichever grunt Sullivan chose to ship the heroin home with, it had to happen before the whole team was killed—certainly before Sullivan was blinded."

"Or maybe," Jaworski countered, "he picked somebody not on his team, from another outfit. Have you thought of that?"

"Well, whoever is digging up graves doesn't think so," Lonto replied. "Maybe they know something we don't."

Jaworski snorted. "They probably know a lot more than we do! Any other leads?"

"All we have, you have."

"I do follow what you've said, but digging up graves is going to stir up a lot of shit."

"Boss, there's a lot of other shit in one of those graves, maybe enough to cover the city."

"Yeah," Jaworski agreed, "that's the only reason I'm going to go along with this grave-digging idea. How are you going to handle it?"

The two detectives didn't really want to be the ones who "handled" the matter. They'd have preferred Jaworski to order constant surveillance on Shapiro and McCurdy and to post cops at every cemetery in town. But that was no way to validate their theory. It was only fair that those who came up with the idea should be the ones to implement it. They were still counting on receiving some help from army records so that they might be better able to pin down a grave. But finding these dead men wasn't as easy as stumbling over the other dead people in this case.

At five o'clock that evening, just as they were about to give up on the army, Lonto's phone jolted him out of his despair. "Homicide, Lonto."

"Tony, this is Wolverton on the desk."

"What's up, Sarge?"

"Jimmy Webb is here to see you."

"Who?"

"You know, Blind Jimmy. He says he got word you wanted to see him."

"Have an officer bring him right up!"

"How long has he had the Bible?" Runnion asked.

Lonto glanced at his watch. "Since yesterday."

James Webb was in his early sixties. He wore a light blue summer suit, a pastel shirt, and black loafers. He looked pretty good, but had to accept the word of others for his appearance. His silver hair was well groomed and he wore dark glasses. The scars he had received were faintly visible. He had been hit in the face with a glass of acid when he was a young and upcoming attorney. He now owned a bookstore that specialized in literature and music for his fellow blind people. He appeared eager to talk to Lonto about the Bible.

"Well, Jimmy, anything?"

"Yes, indeed! Although I nearly missed it."

"What happened?"

"I read it, found absolutely nothing unusual about the Bible and was about to put it back into the envelope you had it in when it dawned on me that something was missing."

"Missing?"

"What I mean, Tony, is that I remembered I had forgotten to put the page marker back in the book. It's a leather marker, about two inches wide and maybe eight inches long. When I picked it up from the table to put it in the book, I noticed that there was braille writing on it!"

"On the marker, not in the Bible?"

"Right! Here, look at the smooth side."

Lonto took the strip of leather and turned it over to its smooth side. It was a deep reddish color, and peering very closely, Lonto was able to see tiny bumps. He ran his fingertips over them, a grin spreading across his face. "This is it, Pat!"

Runnion took the strip and ran his fingers across the raised dots. "Yeah. Tooled right into the leather." He held it to the light:

"It's rather crude braille, but anyone who can read braille can make this out easily," Jimmy informed them.

"Then this is the message! What does it say?"

"Well, it's not actually a message in the strict sense. It's a list of Bible chapters and verses."

Lonto handed the strip back to Jimmy, picked up his pen, and pulled a sheet of paper out of his desk drawer. "Read the list to me, Jimmy."

"Okay. Acts 2:1, 1 Samuel 7:1, Acts 9:1, 1 Corinthians 6:1, Revelations 6:1, Amos 5:1, Isaiah 8:1, and Nahum 2:1."

"Jimmy, you've been a great, great help. I don't suppose you had the time to look up the chapters?" Lonto asked hopefully.

"Sure. There's nothing marked in the book under any of them, nothing unusual. In fact, if the owner was a Bible student, his choice of chapters and verses doesn't make a lot of sense."

"Why not?" Runnion asked.

"They're unrelated. They're not very important or meaningful. There's no reason to study them. The only thing it could be is a one-time pad—you know, like spies use. It's the safest code there is. And books are the favorite way to do it. See, the decoder has the same Bible and he knows which words or letters in those verses are used in the code."

"Jimmy, read them to us, will you?"

"Sure, but I warn you, a reading brings nothing out. I'll start in the order I gave them to you. 'And when the day of Pentecost was fully come, they were all with one accord in one place.'

"And the men of Kirjathjearim came, and fetched up the ark of the Lord.'

"'And Saul, yet breathing out threatenings and slaughter against the disciples of the Lord, went unto the high priest.'

"'Dare any of you, having a matter against another, go to law before the unjust, and not before the saints?'

"'And I saw when the Lamb opened one of the seals, and

I heard, as it were the noise of thunder, one of the four beasts saying, Come and see.'

"'Hear ye this word which I take up against you, even a lamentation, O house of Israel.'

"'Moreover the Lord said unto me, Take thee a great roll and write in it with a man's pen concerning Mahershalalhashbaz.'

"And the last one, 'He that dasheth in pieces is come up before thy face: keep the munition, watch the way, make thy loins strong, fortify thy power mightily.'"

Jimmy closed the Bible and placed it on the desk. "Like I said, none of the verses are related to each other."

Lonto and Runnion studied the list and the written verses closely, in mounting frustration. Both were very much aware that what they wanted was right in front of their eyes. Yet they couldn't find it. The verses made no sense to them.

At six o'clock that evening, both men were still at their desks when Detective Mills arrived to relieve them. He casually hung his jacket over the back of a chair and picked up the list of Bible chapters.

"What are you guys doing, Tony? Playing word games or designing codes?"

"What?"

"Asa Crain," Mills said. "Right here." He pointed to the list. "Look at the list. The first letter of each book of the Bible, top to bottom. They spell out Crain's name."

"Give me that," Lonto demanded. He read down the list: Acts, Samuel, Acts, Corinthians, Revelations, Amos, Isaiah, Nahum. Asa Crain! "That's it, Pat! Crain is the one. Mills, you're almost a real detective!"

Mills stood grinning, wondering what the hell Lonto was talking about. Lonto and Runnion each reached for a phone.

11

There were exactly eighty-six Crains in the phone book. At fifty-two they were batting zero, and had fourteen call-backs to make, having received no answer. They were going to start the call-backs in a few minutes, but it wasn't necessary.

On call fifty-three, the home of Albert and Eva Crain, at 1420 Forest Avenue North, in the suburb of Spring Lake, they hit pay dirt. "Mr. Crain? This is Detective Anthony Lonto of the Sixth Precinct. We are investigating a serious matter and need some information."

"Certainly, officer. How can I help you?"

"Did your son die in Vietnam, sir?"

"Why, yes. Yes, he did."

"Was his name Asa Crain?"

"Yes. But he's been gone for years now. Why do you want his name and all?"

"We are involved in a murder investigation, sir, and we have to check certain matters. His name came up as a former friend of the murdered man. Was Asa returned to you by the army?"

"Yes. They took him from us young and gave him back dead."

"Was Asa buried in this city?"

"Yes, here in Spring Lake, at Oak Hills Memorial Gardens."

"Thank you Mr. Crain. You've been most helpful. I am sorry that I had to disturb your evening and bring up painful memories.

"Pat! I've got it. Oak Hills Memorial Gardens in Spring Lake."

"So, we stake out a cemetery?"

"Yeah. I hope none of our boys are superstitious."

A police stakeout is a boring event. Long hours of waiting, filled with lukewarm coffee in styrofoam cups, stale cigarettes, and sore asses. A stakeout for surveillance purposes results in a simple report. If the stakeout is designed, as was this one, to spot and arrest suspects, the results are either violent or dull.

A graveyard stakeout has to be the most boring of all. It is forbidden even to move about, lest the suspect see you instead of you him.

The cemetery that night was still and humid, the day's heat retained by the earth. As Lonto and Runnion sat watching, they noticed a ground fog creeping across the grass. Runnion turned to Lonto. "Listen, man, if some sonofabitch wearing a fucking cape comes out of that fog, I'm gone!"

Lonto chuckled. "It does look like a midnight horror flick, doesn't it?"

Neither man was inordinately superstitious, but dark and foggy cemeteries tend to awaken the atavistic consciousness of humanity's earliest days. They noticed a subtle dryness in

164

their mouths as they squirmed into more comfortable positions. They were not afraid, but they were apprehensive with the knowledge that violence might well be imminent. They were quiet, crouched down, looking, in the shadows, like two tombstones.

Grave-robbing is a slow and tedious business, and an impatient man is most affected by the slow passage of time. Julian Shapiro was not a patient man. It was not the time creeping by that provoked his impatience, but the thought of millions of dollars just under the earth in front of him. He simply couldn't wait to get his hands on the heroin and complete the wholesale deal he had made with two of the city's major heroin dealers. He was near his reward, after dealing with that asshole Baratto for a couple of years, after the waiting, after the risks, after the killing of the prostitute and Baratto. The time was near when the payoff would be his.

He shifted from one foot to the other at the edge of the grave, and stared intently into the pit. Deep in the black hole, McCurdy was busy digging. "Jesus, Frank. Can you dig faster? The waiting is killing me!"

"Almost there, boss. Another few minutes and I'll be able to pry it open. A couple of minutes and we'll be rich."

Shapiro knelt at the head of the grave and pointed his small penlight into the gaping hole. He shielded the glare with his other hand, took it away to see if his gun was still in place in his pocket, and again shielded the light. He was staring at McCurdy's head. No, Frank, he thought. Not *we*, just me.

Runnion first spotted the tiny flash of light when Shapiro had felt for his gun. He nudged Lonto. Lonto nodded; he had seen it, too. "Move in slowly and put the light on them when I give the word," he whispered into Runnion's ear.

It was going very smoothly, Lonto thought. Mills and another detective, O'Malley, were in position on the other side of the Crain grave. Lonto whispered into the walkie-talkie, ordering them to move in slowly. He and Runnion did the same. Lonto smiled to himself. They would scare the shit out of Shapiro! And they would catch him and McCurdy as dirty as a cop can ever catch anyone.

Shapiro wasn't cooperating in the manner the police had anticipated, however. He was in the process of terminating his long association with Frank McCurdy. He was going to place a bullet in McCurdy's head. He fired just as Lonto yelled.

"Police! Freeze, and keep your hands in sight! Freeze!"

Lonto and Runnion saw the flash just as Runnion was hitting the switch of the flashlight. They thought either Shapiro or McCurdy was firing on them. They returned the fire. Mills and O'Malley joined in, and for four or five seconds there was an ear-shattering firefight ending with a scream and a thud as Shapiro landed on the coffin of Asa Crain.

"Anyone hit?" shouted Lonto.

"We're okay over here, Tony," Mills shouted. "You two okay?"

"Yeah, we're all right," Runnion announced.

They moved cautiously toward the Crain plot, guns pointed in the direction of the gaping hole, the flashlight casting an eerie glow over all. Seeing and hearing nothing, they came to the edge of the grave and looked down. Shapiro and McCurdy, the partners, were united in death as they had been in life—Shapiro was on top, his blood mingling with McCurdy's.

The four detectives, almost in unison, backed away from the open wound in the earth, recoiling from the combined stench of blood, cordite, sweat, fear, and old death.

"Call it in and get a wagon here," Lonto ordered.

It was a long night. McCurdy was dead, killed by the shot that had ignited the firefight. Shapiro, to their surprise, was still alive and was rushed to the nearest hospital. He had taken at least three slugs in the upper body. Runnion and Lonto didn't think he'd last through the night.

In the emergency room, in the presence of several doctors and nurses and a police attorney, Shapiro told them about the five kilograms of pure heroin he was now dying for. He gave them the whole story. His tenuous grip on life had seemed to transform him from the closemouthed tough guy of yesterday into a cooperative witness, almost as though he were an innocent party to the events he described.

"Baratto told us all about it when he got back from Vietnam. I really didn't believe him, but then the punk brought us some samples. God, it was the greatest smack I ever seen! Him and Sullivan both had brought back small pieces in the bottom of their duffel bags. . . . Doc, am I gonna make it?"

"Frankly, it's too early to say, Mr. Shapiro. We're doing everything we can."

"Yeah, listen, I appreciate it, Doc. Don't let me die."

"What happened next, Julian?" Lonto asked him.

"Well, Leo didn't know where the shit was. Only Sullivan knew which coffin the smack was in. Being blind had gotten to Sullivan, he was mean and suspicious and wouldn't tell Leo shit about the dope." He coughed and a fine mist of blood flew from his lips, which were becoming bluish.

"He finally got out of the hospital a few weeks ago, and Leo told him he was being pressured by us for the money we had loaned him. He tried to make Sullivan act right, but the guy told Leo to fuck off, they'd get the smack when he, Sullivan, said so. Leo got carried away and ended up killing the guy."

"Who stumbled on where it was?" Runnion asked him.

"Baratto had an idea all along, and I guess Sullivan said something to make Leo think he knew. Leo said it must be in the grave of one of his army pals. It was."

"Who whacked Baratto?"

"McCurdy," Shapiro said promptly. "Who needed the

167

punk after he told us all he knew? We knew it was in one of four graves. Shit, I wasn't going to buy it from him to begin with! I wanted it all," Shapiro finished. He sighed and turned his eyes on the doctor. Before he could speak, his eyes closed.

"That's it, gentlemen. He's gone."

Later, in Jaworski's office, the lieutenant read the confession and the full report of Lonto and Runnion. When he finished, he laid the documents on the desk, next to a dirty and blood-spattered package wrapped in heavy-duty cellophane. Then he spoke, quietly. "There's millions of dollars right in this little package. Millions."

"It is expensive, all right, Lieutenant. It cost the lives of five people that we know of. Real expensive shit."

Jaworski leaned back in his chair and clasped his hands behind his head. "You two did pretty well on this case. In fact, you did a hell of a good job."

Lonto and Runnion exchanged looks at each other and then turned to Jaworski. Before they could speak, Jaworski beat them to the punch. "Don't let that go to your heads. Get the hell out of here and get to work. Wait, it's fucking midnight! Go home, clean up and rest and take two days off, just two days."

"Gee," Runnion said, after they closed the door to Jaworski's office behind them. "Two days off! The rewards of being a hero!"

"Want to get drunk?" Lonto asked him.

"Why not?" Runnion said, holding the station house door open and waving Lonto through. They walked side by side, grinning.